THE EDGE OF THE WORLD

GARRETT LEIGH

PRAISE FOR GARRETT LEIGH

"Emotional and brilliant..."

ALL ABOUT ROMANCE

"Tastefully erotic ... more smart than smutty..."

PUBLISHERS WEEKLY

"Powerful and compelling..."

FOREWORD REVIEWS

CHAPTER ONE

SHAY MALONEY poured himself onto the plush couch at the back of the tour bus. "How does this even happen?" he wondered aloud. "We're a pirate band from Derby."

Corina, his manager and instigator of Smuggler's Beat's meteoric rise from pub band to touring megalodon—in folk music terms, at least—flicked an impatient eyebrow. "Hard work. Yours and mine. Don't start being a brat about it now."

Brat. The term set Shay's teeth on edge. At twenty-three, he'd outgrown the child prodigy label he'd carried through school, but the word still stung. He flung his feet up on the seat. "I need new boots."

Corina didn't reply.

A little while later, they rolled into Dublin, the first stop on the tour. The band shuffled off the bus in various states of disarray after seven hours on the road. Shay was the only one without a hangover, by laziness rather than design—the fridge was at the front of the bus.

Backstage at the venue, they decamped to the dressing room. It was the most luxurious they'd had so far but still amounted to little more than a couch too small for five people, a can of Pringles, and the world's smallest telly. Shay wasn't complaining, though; he had no time to lounge around. His pregig routine was sacred, and even a rough ferry voyage and some dodgy tuna sandwiches wouldn't keep him from his solitary circuit of the unfamiliar stage.

He escaped the rest of the band at the first opportunity and ventured along a dark corridor. The three-thousand capacity indie club was a big name to have on their scorecard, but in reality, the grand venue was pretty dingy behind the scenes. Gig detritus cluttered every corner, and it smelled like an old man's empty wallet.

Shay picked his way through until he found the stage. Finally, the magic hit. Wooden and weathered, high ceilings and sticky floors, the venue was everything he'd ever dreamed of beyond the muddy festivals the band had spent their entire summer frequenting. Rock and pop could keep their stadiums and arenas. For Shay, *this* was everything.

As was his habit, he lay down on the stage and closed his eyes, imagining how it would feel when the lights went down. When the sold-out crowd would either love them or hate them. Smuggler's Beat had a loyal following, but their eclectic shanty-punk vibe was an acquired taste, and it was hard to ever feel at home in a city they'd never played before. Their record company had taken a chance on them, and the mantra that followed them around was stronger nowhere than in Shay's own head. *What if we fucking bomb?*

"Then you'll be out on your ear and back to being an accountant, or whatever it is you posh kids do when you get back on the straight and narrow."

Shay jumped and opened one eye to face Larry, the grizzled percussionist who was the heartbeat to Shay's lyrical soul. "Accountant? I barely got GCSEs, I'm from the arse crack of Derby, and I haven't ever been straight."

"There's still time," Larry deadpanned. "Though I don't know what you're worried about. These are your people, aren't they?"

"Who?"

Larry rolled his eyes. "The Irish, knobhead. That's why we

came here... to bookend the tour with our fearless leader's heritage, Dublin to Derby."

He wandered off, saving Shay the trouble of another retort, and Shay stared after him, long-carried disquiet fizzing gently in his already nervous heart. *Your people.* Yeah, right. If only he knew Shay's name was a lie and he had no more Gaelic blood in him than Cuban-born Larry.

SHOWTIME. OLLIE Pietruska stood in the press booth of the packed venue and observed Smuggler's Beat as they took to the stage. The Cuban drummer, the chiselled fiddler. The dreadlocked bass player, and the pianist with her long white hair. And the reason Ollie had braved a Ryanair flight across the Irish Sea bounced out behind them. All alabaster-skinned, chestnut-haired, six foot of him.

Ollie sighed. *Fuck's sake.* Somehow, despite the mad-panicked month he'd spent researching this man, he hadn't got round to digging up a photograph of his present-day self—or actually, any photographs of him at all. He knew what the bloke's grandfather looked like, his great-aunt, and his long-lost distant cousin, but until this moment, Shay Maloney had been nothing more than a name begrudgingly scrawled on the first page of a brand-new notebook.

Now he was a vision in skintight jeans and battered boots, chin-length hair tucked under a leather fedora, and a vintage guitar slung over his shoulder. Everything Ollie had ever dreamed of when his imagination got the better of him. Goddammit, Shay Maloney was *gorgeous.*

Ollie cursed again and leaned on the railing as Smuggler's Beat launched into their first song, an upbeat ceilidh number with a tribal twist. The band was famed for their fusion folk style, but Ollie had neglected to research that, too, so was sorely unprepared for the pulsing, grinding rhythm that seeped, unbidden, into his bones. Smuggler's Beat were... awesome, and it was quite clear to Ollie that their secret lay in the indomitable charisma of their dazzling frontman.

The band churned out song after song, each laced with their trademark energy but distinctly different from the one that came before. They were the Aladdin's cave of folk music—a genre Ollie had assumed to be dull—and it wasn't long before the confines of the press booth became too much.

Gaze fixed on the stage, Ollie slipped out of the booth and down the steps into the crowd. The singer was playing a bright melody on a harmonica, all the while stomping his booted feet to a rhythm that drove the audience wild.

They stomped along with him, moving like a beer-fuelled ocean. The real ale being served at the bar slopped onto the floor, and as Shay swapped his harmonica for an accordion, they roared.

Goosebumps broke out over Ollie's skin, tingling in places, a phantom sting creeping across others, as though his ruined body had never healed. Irritated, he rubbed his arms and swept the stage again, searching for a welcome distraction.

The band had evolved in the brief moment Ollie had been gone. Instruments had been swapped around, and they'd moved to the front of the stage. Shay Maloney held a drum Ollie couldn't name, and even from a distance, Ollie saw the mischief in his eyes.

He took the mic. "We're gonna have some fun now. Bring the house down before we let you go home."

The crowd booed their dismay at the prospect of the rowdy gig coming to an end, but Ollie barely heard it, instead inexplicably lost in the melodic lilt of Maloney's Derbyshire accent. For some reason, he'd expected Irish brogue, even though Ollie knew there was nothing Irish about the entrancing singer.

I wonder if he knows too. But Ollie nixed the thought before it took hold and roused the detective part of his brain. What Shay knew about himself right now was irrelevant. By the end of the tour, he'd know it all, and then Ollie could go home. *Fuck this shit.*

As though he'd somehow heard Ollie's rebellion, Shay shifted his gaze, scoping out the crowd until he seemed to be staring right at Ollie. They locked eyes. The world shifted, and Ollie sucked in a breath. His hands were clenched at his sides, but as Shay Maloney held him hostage, the ever-present tension in his body gave way to a feeling he didn't recognise.

A warm tide creeping into a sun-soaked bay.

What the fuck?

But the sensation was gone as fast as it had arrived. As Ollie shook himself, Shay looked away and jumped straight into a jigged-up song that was clearly a fan favourite. There were drums of all kinds, a penny whistle, a violin, and even a banjo. And above it all, Shay Maloney's velvet voice rang out, cloaking the packed concert hall in his magic as Ollie fell under his spell.

The song played out. Calls for an encore were met with another round of the opening number, and then it was over. The band left the stage. Ollie watched them go, noting how Shay was the first to duck behind the curtain, as though it were midnight and he had something to hide.

Ollie snorted. *Wrong way round, dickhead.* And it was true. Shay Maloney had many secrets….

He just didn't know it yet.

CHAPTER TWO

SHAY WOKE with a low groan and a banging headache. Getting shitfaced before a gig was a big no-no, but after? Fucking-A. Beer, vodka, and something sticky that was bound to ruin his day. Worth it, though. He'd come off stage last night off-kilter, as though he'd missed something really fucking important, but at the same time relieved the gig was over, which never happened. *I don't have time for this shit, man.* Who did? Being a weirdo was overrated.

Yawning, Shay stretched, and then immediately regretted it as his leg dropped out of the narrow bunk and chilly air hit his bare skin. *Wow, son.* In the three months leading up to this tour, he'd fantasised about how much fun it would be to live on a tour bus. To sleep in close quarters with his bandmates and share every moment of their dream come true.

The reality was cramped and noisy and smelled like arse.

Fuck's sake. Groaning again, he pulled his tiny pillow over his head. Somewhere someone chuckled and threw a paper cup at him. Awesome. He'd forgotten to pull the curtains too. Not that it would've made much difference. By the racket going on around him, the rest of the world was already wide awake.

He admitted defeat and sat up. Ben—the band's resident fiddle player—was in the bunk opposite, but he was paying Shay no heed, engrossed, as usual, in texting his girlfriend back home. Shay searched further afield for the cup thrower and found Jumbo, the bassist, grinning like a twat.

Shay sighed. "Wanker."

Jumbo laughed. "Mornin'. Or afternoon more like. You get your beauty sleep?"

"Fuck off." Shay scowled and then regretted it as the effort made his head pound. "What time is it?"

"One o'clock. You missed lunch."

Great. Shay's stomach growled. Hung-over or not, he didn't miss meals. Couldn't. With a sigh, he reached for the bag he always kept within arm's reach, no matter how much vodka he'd sunk the night before. He tested his blood sugar, wincing when he saw the result. He needed breakfast, and fast.

As if on cue, Corina appeared, brandishing porridge, a banana, and a Costa cup of something that smelled like grass. "Sort your-self out, Maloney. You've got a busy day."

"Yes, Ma."

"Watch it."

She disappeared, leaving Shay to jab some insulin into his belly and scarf his breakfast. When he was done, Larry came to sit with him. His comforting bulk was soothing. Everyone leaned on Larry. Even Shay, who found the concept of leaning on anyone mildly disturbing. He dozed with his head lolled on Larry's shoulder for a while, until Corina returned to drag him away.

They'd stopped in Athlone, the midway point between Dublin and Galway. Shay peered out of the windows at the front of the bus. Corina nudged him hard in the ribs.

"If you wanted to sightsee, you should've gone to bed earlier. Sit down. We've got things to do."

Shay thought about muttering something derogatory under his breath but bottled it when he sensed the weight of Corina's glare. She was a slave driver with little patience for anything that messed with her meticulous schedule, but beyond that, she was a bloody good manager. Without her, Smuggler's Beat would still be playing workingmen's clubs. Besides, she was right. No one had *made* him stay up late in a futile attempt to drink more vodka than Russian-born Mara—the band's hollow-legged pianist.

The front of the bus housed a kitchen area and a makeshift office space. Shay took a seat at the table and resisted the urge to slump forwards like a child and rest his head on his arms. His daily self-care routine had fixed his blood sugar, but he was still hanging.

Corina plonked a coffee in front of him. "Buck up, kiddo. I wasn't joking when I said you have a busy day."

"What's so busy about it?" Shay drew the coffee towards him. "Apart from the obvious. You didn't book more TV slots, did you? I hate that shit."

"Why? You don't mind being on stage."

"That's not the same thing. We play live on stage, and we sound good. TV fucks everything up."

Corina treated him to a rare smile. "That's life, Shay. But no, I haven't booked you on to any *more* TV shows. This one is something you've already agreed to, and it's not actually about the band."

"Huh?"

"It's the genealogy documentary, remember? I told you ages ago that a researcher would be coming to take you through what they found out about you and film it for Sky Arts."

Corina had a habit of springing things on Shay first thing in the morning when he didn't know which way was up. Who the hell knew what he'd agreed to when he'd been half-asleep. This, though, rang a distant and unwelcome bell. "My ma was dying of cancer when you asked me about this. I'd have told you anything to get rid of you."

"Then you should've told me no," Corina retorted, not unkindly. "I'd never force you into something you didn't want to do, but I can't get you out of things you've already agreed to just because you've forgotten about them and then subsequently changed your mind. Not with players as big as Sky."

She was right, and Shay remembered now why he'd agreed to film the documentary. His ma had wanted him to. *"Your dad and I*

*aren't all you are, sunshine. Let these people do some legwork for you...
and take from it whatever you need."*

Shay sighed. Take from it whatever you need? What if he
didn't need anything? What if he was perfectly content with life
as it was? Des and Michelle Maloney had lost their own parents
long before Shay had come along, but they'd given him a home so
full of life and love he'd never missed the big families some of his
mates had grown up with. Why—

"Shay?"

"Hmm?"

Corina pushed a piece of paper towards him. "You need to
sign this."

"What is it?"

"The nondisclosure agreement between you and Sky. It means
the researcher won't report anything he sees on tour."

"On tour?"

"Yes." Corina drummed her nails on the table. "I *told* you this
before we hit the road. The researcher is joining the tour and
filming the documentary as we go. This is *happening,* Shay. And it
starts today."

***

OLLIE SHIFTED his weight from one foot to the other, his bag at his
feet. Ditching his hire car and getting the train to Galway had
eased his frayed nerves a little, but he still didn't relish the
prospect of a month trapped on the Smuggler's Beat tour bus. The
only consolation was he'd seen firsthand that the band had
serious talent. The one thing worse than being stuck on a never-
ending work trip would be if it were accompanied by a shit
soundtrack.

Actually, Ollie could think of plenty of reasons why the next
five weeks would suck, but he'd run out of time to imagine the
worst. A beast of a bus with blacked-out windows rolled into the
car park. Shay Maloney had arrived.

The bus parked and the doors opened. People began to spill

down the steps. Ollie recognised a few band members, but there was no sign of the man he'd spent a night in a dingy Premier Inn trying to forget. Or rather, trying to put back in a box that was entirely professional. Shay Maloney had been on his mind for weeks and would remain so for the foreseeable future. He could do without the dirty daydreams.

Honest.

A woman with an iPad and a briefcase got off the bus. As she was the only one who didn't look as though she'd just fallen out of the pub, Ollie took her to be his contact at Folklore Records, Corina Hussain. *Here goes nothing.*

He picked up his bag and crossed the car park. She saw him coming and met him halfway.

"Ollie Pietruska? From Sky?"

He shrugged. "I'm a freelancer, but whatever."

Corina Hussain was not amused. Her sharp eyes narrowed, and her grip on her iPad tightened. "Are you here to film the genealogy documentary with Shay Maloney?"

"Um. Yes."

"Good. I'm going to let the band get settled in the venue, then I'll take you to meet him. In the meantime, why don't you take a look around the bus? Your bunk is at the back by the lounge."

She walked away without waiting for an answer. Lacking any better ideas, Ollie boarded the bus to find it empty. Somehow, in the thirty seconds he'd spent with Corina, he'd missed the rest of the band disembarking, and an odd disappointment tickled his chest. *Idiot. You'll be sick of them all by the end of the day.* But still. The bus smelled like most buses did when they were home to a dozen people, but there was something else in the air too.

Excitement?

Nah. It couldn't be. Despite the spine-tingling gig the night before, Ollie had taken this assignment under duress, and the sooner it was over, the better... right?

Two hours later and Ollie was already at home with his rejuvenated pessimism. The Wi-Fi on the bus didn't work, there was no nearby plug socket for his laptop, and his bunk was little more than a padded shelf. Also, not a soul had returned to the bus since the Smuggler's Beat crew had disappeared into the venue, meaning that he hadn't even begun to unpick the complex task of solo filming an entire documentary.

"The rawness of the filming is the beauty of the series," his producer had said. *"And no one does it better than you."*

Easy for him to say. He wasn't the mug with nothing but a Sony a7S II and some other half-arsed equipment in his bag.

Ollie abandoned his bunk and took a tour of the bus. It was flashy in all the right places, but beyond the shiny chrome and coloured lights, it was pretty basic. A kitchen, a tiny bathroom, the bunks, and a lounge with a couch that ran around the entire back of the bus. Ollie walked up and down the aisle and wondered which bunk was Shay Maloney's. Was it the one covered in balled-up socks and crisp packets? Or the one with the photo of a beautiful blonde on the pillow?

Or maybe it was the bed that looked as though it hadn't been slept in. Neat as a pin, the only signs of life were a weathered leather-bound notebook, a pencil, and a small black wash bag.

The nosy bastard in Ollie itched to pick up the notebook and leaf through the pages, to intrude on the private thoughts of whoever it belonged to, but he sensed a presence behind him before the little boy who knew to mind his own business won out, and he spun around.

Shay Maloney stood behind him, somehow filling the narrow aisle with his slender frame, his gorgeous features resting in the kind of bored expression Ollie expected from overindulged rock stars. "Are you the bloke from Sky?"

Ollie resisted the urge to repeat his freelancer status and stuck out his hand with a brisk nod, trying to ignore the voice in his head screaming that Shay Maloney was even more beautiful in person than he had been on a distant stage. "Yup. I'm Ollie. I'm going to be with your tour, off and on, until we get to the end."

"The end?"

"Yes… of your tour or the filming. Whichever happens first."

Shay finally took Ollie's hand. He closed his elegant fingers around Ollie's with a brief, intense squeeze that made Ollie's tongue stick to the roof of his mouth. "You don't know how long it will take?"

Ollie swallowed. "Not exactly. I only took the assignment a month ago. I haven't finished your story yet."

Shay let his hand drop, a frown creasing his smooth forehead. He pushed his hair back, tucking it behind his ears, and slumped against the bathroom door with a sigh. "I figured you'd have it all today, that we could read through it and do whatever big reveal you had in mind. Get it over with."

"I take it you didn't watch the first series when it aired last year, then?"

"Dude, I don't even know what the series is called. My manager made me sign shit when I was distracted."

Great. Ollie had taken this project at the last minute, and he had spent many sleepless nights unravelling the mess of leads the original researcher had left behind, but despite all that, he hadn't accounted for Shay's apathy. "You don't want to do it?"

Shay shrugged. "Does it matter?"

Ollie didn't have an answer for that. "Whatever. How long have you got before soundcheck?"

"An hour."

"That'll do. Take a seat, and I'll show you what I have in mind."

CHAPTER THREE

SHAY TAPPED his fingers on the desk. It was the second occasion that day he'd found himself trapped in the office with a pile of paperwork, but this time, his hostage taker was having a far more profound effect on him than Corina ever had.

Ollie pointed at his laptop screen. They were watching an old episode from the genealogy series Shay had unwittingly agreed to take part in. "I didn't film this one, but it was produced on the road, like I'm planning to do with you, so it gives you a good idea of what to expect."

"Uh-huh." Shay tried to focus on the screen, but there was something about the dude across the table that wouldn't let him. With his dark stubble and flinty eyes, ripped jeans and leather jacket, Ollie Pietruska looked more like a rock star than anyone on the tour, and yet there was something so unassuming about him that the contradiction had Shay totally fucking fascinated.

'Course it didn't help that the bloke was bloody gorgeous. Inky hair, *that stubble*, beautiful hands. And God, his voice. He had a London accent, fused with something Shay couldn't quite put his finger on. "Where's your accent from?"

Ollie muted the video. "Sorry, what?"

"Your accent," Shay repeated. "It's not English."

Ollie's gaze darted somewhere beyond Shay and back again so

fast Shay was almost sure he'd imagined it. "It's Polish, like my name. I lived in Warsaw for about ten years when I was a kid and then in Waltham, West London, after that, so I'm a bit of a mix."

"I like it."

Ollie's left eyebrow twitched. "Um, thanks, I guess? We're not really here to talk about me."

Shame. Shay had been trapped in the studio recording back-to-back albums for most of the year and had then hit the road for a mad summer of festivals and underground gigs. Another two months in the studio, and now he was living on a bus. Many faces had come and gone, but none had turned his head like Ollie. In fact, Shay couldn't remember ever being so immediately and entirely entranced by someone... particularly someone who didn't seem to want to look at him.

Shay studied Ollie's profile, taking in his high cheekbones and intense stare as he cued up another clip of the genealogy show. *I bet he's got a killer smile.* Then again, he didn't seem the type to smile much, and Shay liked that too. Smuggler's Beat was his happy place, a manic joy he couldn't escape. Inexplicably, he craved Ollie's frown.

"So...." Ollie said.

"Hmm?"

A muscle in Ollie's cheek ticked. "You're really not interested in this, are you?"

"We haven't started yet."

"That's what you're going with? Because I don't need to waste my time with this. We can just film the segments on the road whenever you're free and leave it at that. You don't have to be involved with production."

"Production?"

"Jesus-fucking-Christ."

Shay blinked, caught off guard by the irritation lacing Ollie's curse. He searched for a response, but the words wouldn't come. His hands trembled, and a faint headache crept over his scalp. *Shit.* He'd forgotten to check his sugars and top up his breakfast. A night on the booze always fucked him up.

Ollie was still glaring at him. Shay forced himself to shift his gaze and glanced around for his medicine bag. It was, of course, on his bunk, an easy reach when his limbs weren't made of jelly.

"Are you okay?"

"Wha—" Shay tried to stand. Failed. Strong hands caught him and sat him back down with a thump. "Oh fuck."

"What's wrong?" Suddenly, Ollie was right in front of him, crouched at his feet, his previously steely eyes now molten with concern. "Do you need me to get someone?"

Shay shook his head. "I just need my bag. I'm diabetic... I need to check my sugars."

"Where's the bag?"

"On my bed."

"The tidy one with the journal?"

"Yeah."

"Of course it is."

Ollie rose and disappeared, returning an instant later with Shay's magic bag. He stayed close as Shay pricked his finger, but looked away as the drop of blood oozed out.

Shay filed the reaction for later and concentrated on the less than ideal numbers coming up on the tiny device on the table. "Oops."

"What is it?"

"Low. I need some sugar, man."

"What kind of sugar?"

"Coke... maybe some fruit?"

Thankfully, both things were stocked in the kitchen. Ollie brought him a can of Pepsi and a banana and reclaimed his seat as Shay put himself back together. Shay mourned the loss of his close proximity, but it took a few minutes for him to notice Ollie was furtively scribbling in a notebook of his own.

"Please tell me you're not documenting this shit?"

"Hmm?" It was Ollie's turn to glance up distractedly. "Sorry. No, of course I'm not, but I didn't know you were diabetic. It's... uh... interesting to me. I didn't mean to offend you."

"I'm pretty hard to offend, mate. But I don't see what's so interesting about me fucking up a hangover."

"That's because you haven't listened to anything I've said for the past hour. Maybe if you pay attention over the next few weeks, it'll make more sense."

"That's what *you're* going with?"

Finally, Ollie cracked a smile, and it was bright enough to break the hypo-haze clouding Shay's vision. "I'm not going with anything. I'm here doing my thing, and you're doing yours. How much the two cross over is up to you."

The statement seemed to answer a question Shay hadn't asked. He swallowed the last bite of banana and folded the peel into a neat pile. "Are you saying you want me involved in production, or you'd rather I left you alone to get on with it?"

"I'm saying it's up to you. It doesn't matter to me, mate. I'm just doing my job."

An odd disappointment swept over Shay. Ollie's cool demeanour had returned as fast as Shay's cognition, but he hadn't considered that Ollie's work might be nothing more than a pay cheque to him. In Shay's world, pretty much everyone except the bus driver was emotionally shackled to their job. Even Corina. Especially Corina. "How far back have you gone?"

"With your family tree?"

Shay guzzled more Pepsi. "Yeah. I mean, I know my ma had some pretty cool artists in her family, and my dad's brothers were all pilots, so…." Shay broke off as the weight of Ollie's stare hit him. "What?"

Ollie closed his laptop, his perpetual frown deepening. "I think there's been a misunderstanding here."

"What do you mean?"

"I mean about what we're doing." Ollie reached down and drew a thick folder of papers from his bag. He laid them on the table and spun it so Shay could see the first page. At the top was a name Shay didn't recognise. Ollie tapped his finger on it. "Shay, I'm not researching your adoptive family. I'm researching *you*."

GUILT WASN'T an emotion Ollie had expected to deal with when he'd agreed to take on the Shay Maloney project at the eleventh hour, but it was hard not to feel bad for Shay. He'd had all of ten seconds to react to Ollie's unwitting bombshell before he'd been called away, and he'd left the bus with his lovely face twisted in a painful combination of shock and confusion.

Jesus Christ. Ollie fired off a rapid text to his producer in London.

Ollie: *I thought Maloney knew he was adopted?*

Amir: *He does, according to the record company. That's it, though. I'm not sure the kid even knows his birth name.*

With a low growl, Ollie tossed his phone aside. *Shit, shit, shit.* More guilt. It had been clear since he'd set eyes on Shay that afternoon that he'd been walking blind into this project, but to not even realise the Irish roots of his adoptive parents were totally fucking irrelevant? Damn. Someone had some explaining to do, and with Ollie the only idiot on the ground, chances were it would have to be him.

Ollie pulled Shay's file towards him. In the hour that had passed since Shay's manager had hustled him out for soundcheck, it had remained where Shay left it—stacked and heavy and stuck on the first page. Ollie leafed through a few generations until he came to a photograph of Shay's great-uncle. The young man had short hair and a thick beard, but his willowy build was unmistakable. From his never-ending legs to his elegant hands, clutched around a battered cart rattle, he was Shay. Or Shay was him. Or perhaps it was neither, as Shay's name was something else entirely. Ollie traced Shay's birth name and more regret lanced his chest. Ollie had been to hell and back, but he'd always had the luxury of knowing where he'd come from. His roots were absolute. He couldn't imagine how his life would be without a tangible connection to his heritage.

He closed his eyes, and the folk music of his youth echoed in his head, the traditional dances and mystic chants. The smell of his grandmother's cooking and his grandfather's pipe. Who would he be without it?

<hr />

OLLIE FOUND Shay outside the venue. He was alone and leaning against a tree, staring out over the River Corrib. It was such an image, Ollie trailed to a stop, unsure of how to approach him. Or even if he wanted to. Shay had the air of a man who didn't want to be disturbed, and perhaps Ollie was the last person he wanted to see.

A cigarette called Ollie's name. He lit up his first smoke of a very long day and ventured closer to Shay. The click of the lighter seemed to carry on the wind, and Shay turned as Ollie was blowing smoke into the sky.

His expression was unreadable. Ollie considered walking on by, but Shay jerked his head at the last moment, signalling for Ollie to join him.

Wordlessly, he plucked the cigarette from Ollie's hand and took a deep drag. "Come to check out the gig? See what we're all about?"

"Actually, no. I saw you play in Dublin last night."

"That right?" Shay took down another lungful of smoke before handing the cigarette back. "And what did you think? Too weird for you?"

"Not at all. I don't think I've ever seen a band play so many instruments at once."

Shay laughed, a low, short sound that was like a gravelly wind chime. "That's my fault. I collect them and insist on dragging them everywhere we go. The roadies hate me."

"I'm sure they don't. It must make a change from the ordinary."

"You don't like the ordinary?"

It was a strange question, and once more Ollie found himself without an answer. He puffed on his smoke and offered it to Shay again, grinning when he grimaced and shook his head. "Retired smoker, eh?"

"For a long time now. Only relapse when my brain explodes."

It was Ollie's turn to grimace. "Yeah, about that. Sorry I dropped it on you. I kind of assumed you knew… that someone would've told you long before I got here."

"It would make sense." Shay shoved his hands in his pockets. "And maybe they did. I have a habit of not listening to people when I have other shit on my mind. Like, they think I'm hearing them because I'm good at pretending, but in reality I can miss the world ending if I'm involved enough in something else."

"Curse of the creative?"

"Not really. My mum was dying when I agreed to do this, so perhaps the world did end."

Grief flashed in Shay's hazel eyes. The silver ring he wore in his nose glinted in the light from a nearby streetlamp, and a ridiculous urge to comfort him swept over Ollie. *Bet he'd love that after you were the one to torpedo his day right before a massive gig.*

Ollie finished his smoke, stubbed it out, and flicked it into a nearby bin. He stepped closer to Shay, his hands twitching. "I really am sorry. I can speak to the producers, maybe see if we can swap to your adoptive family? They sound interesting too."

Shay shook his head. "I already had it out with Corina. Your studio only wanted me because I was adopted… like that makes history more juicy, or some shit, I don't fucking know. Either way, I signed the contract this morning, so it doesn't matter now."

"Contracts don't mean you don't have choices." But it sounded hollow even to Ollie. He'd signed a contract too, and he wasn't in a position to forfeit the fees that came with it.

Shay sighed. "It's whatever at this point, but do you mind if we hold off starting until I talk to my dad? It feels wrong to be diving into something like this without telling him."

"Of course."

Ollie gave in and laid a hand on Shay's slim shoulder. He kept it there a full second before he wimped out, reclaimed it, and turned away.

Shay caught his arm. "It won't be long. I call him before every gig."

His hot palm burned skin that was already fragile. Ollie stared at where they were joined, his heart thumping. Usually when someone touched him there, by accident or otherwise, nausea would spin him so hard he'd have to make his excuses and split. But something—everything—about Shay was different. His brand of heat didn't hurt, and Ollie was mesmerised by it.

"Of course," he said again. "Come and find me when you're ready."

CHAPTER FOUR

OLLIE WAS unhappy. Shay didn't know how he knew, but he did. The bus was rumbling its way from Galway to Belfast, and most of its occupants were asleep, spent from an amazing gig that had run an hour over schedule.

But Shay was awake, and so was Ollie.

Shay sat up, careful not to whack his head on the low ceiling above his bed. Everyone else had the curtains pulled around their bunks, hiding everything but the sound of Jumbo not so quietly messing around with the girl he'd picked up after the show. But too wired to sleep, Shay had left his open, a decision he regretted now his gaze was fixed on Ollie hunched over a table at the front of the bus. Tense shoulders, restless hands, the bloke was bleeding discomfort, but Shay didn't know why and didn't rate the chances of that changing. Ollie Pietruska was a closed book, and the only reliable emotion Shay had been able to glean from him was a vague irritation.

And he still hadn't figured out why it bothered him so much. Why *Ollie* bothered him so much.

He swung his legs out of his bunk and planted his feet on the unsteady aisle. Irish roads were rocky in places, and he had to hold on to the column walls to keep himself upright as he ventured towards the front of the bus.

The columns ran out just before the kitchen. Shay stumbled the last few steps to the table and crashed into the coffee maker. The noise was enough for Larry to yell out a Cuban curse, but Ollie didn't react. Shay was practically on top of him when he finally glanced up and nearly jumped out of his skin.

"Shit!" He tugged earbuds Shay hadn't noticed out of his ears. "You fucker."

Shay dropped into the seat opposite. "Sorry. Thought you'd hear me coming, I made enough racket."

Ollie stared at him as though he were a mutant. His tousled hair was wilder than Shay had seen it so far, like he'd run his hands through it over and over, and his mystical grey eyes were rimmed with red, signalling the late hour.

Shay suddenly regretted invading his space. There was work paraphernalia—Ollie's work, at least—spread over the table, and Ollie's fingers were wrapped tightly around a pen, a notebook open in front of him. *Fuck, he's not upset, you goon. He's busy.*

But even as the thought crossed Shay's mind, he knew his instincts had been right the first time. He didn't know Ollie from Adam, but something about him right now seemed… off.

Out of habit, Shay jiggled his legs around, rhythm tapping through his veins even when his body was bone tired. His knee brushed what he assumed to be Ollie's. A jolt ran through him, and he shifted again, but this time his thigh found itself pressed against a warmth he couldn't bring himself to abandon yet. He left his leg where it was. Ollie would move if he didn't like it, right?

Ollie didn't move. Didn't blink. Illuminated by a single light in the kitchen, the table was cast in a warm glow. For a long minute, it seemed as though they'd dropped off the edge of the world together. Then Ollie cleared his throat, and the moment passed.

Shay reclaimed his leg, moving it barely a millimetre, but it felt like an inexplicable mile-wide chasm. *Boy, you need to get some sleep.*

"Can't sleep?" Ollie said, as though he'd read Shay's mind.

"Not yet. Sometimes takes me a while if I don't get drunk after a gig. What about you?"

Ollie shrugged. "I'm not used to lying on a bed that's moving."

"You don't like it."

It wasn't a question, but Ollie shook his head anyway. "I prefer my bedroom static."

"Seems legit. But you get used to it after a while, honest."

"I guess we'll see. How are you, anyway? Do you need anything? Drink? Something to eat."

"Don't you fucking start with that shit." Shay reached across the table and gently flicked Ollie's forehead. "I've been diabetic since I was four years old. I can look after myself."

A ghost of a grin warmed Ollie's face. "Fair enough. What can I do for you, then? Are you ready to talk?"

"Actually, yeah. I spoke to my dad, but I don't want to bother you if you're busy."

"I could do with the distraction as it goes." Ollie's grin faded, and left him seeming as tired and rattled as he had from behind. "Where do you want to start?"

"At the beginning?"

Ollie's grin returned, and he shook his head. "Nah, son. The best stories don't go in order."

"So you're not going to tell me who I am? Where my name comes from?"

Ollie leaned back in his seat and folded his arms loosely across his chest. "Not yet. If I'd known you were coming into this blind, I might not have told you what your name even was until the very end."

"Is this a game to you?" The question sounded more loaded than Shay had meant it to, but Ollie seemed to relish intensity, regardless of where it came from.

Like now as he tilted his head sideways and studied Shay across the table, curiosity and speculation making his grey eyes glitter. "It's not a game, but I do enjoy uncovering someone's history, puzzle piece by puzzle piece. And if you don't reveal the obvious answers in the beginning, the end picture is somehow… I don't know, clearer, I suppose."

"You sound mad clever when you say shit like that. Sure you ain't a professor or something?"

Ollie chuckled. "As a working class London boy, I'll take that, but no, I'm nowhere close to being a professor. My degree is shit because I spent most of my uni years smoking weed and drinking rum."

"Worked out okay, though, didn't it?"

"If you say so." Ollie's eyes clouded again. "Anyway. To answer your question, no, I'm not going to tell you where you came from until we get there. I'd like to start in 1864, if that's okay with you."

Shay blinked. "What?"

"In 1864," Ollie repeated as though it made all the sense in the world. "There's a library in Belfast I'd like to go to with you before your gig on Friday. There's some reference books there I want to show you, on camera, but I can give you more details before then if you'd prefer it that way."

Shay chewed on his lip. Being on stage brought him to life in ways he couldn't describe, but cameras made him twitchy. Smuggler's Beat had vowed never to record any videos that weren't live performances, and Shay had never watched any of the YouTube interviews they'd given over the years. The thought alone made him want to die. Could he handle having his arse shown to him with a lens shoved in his face?

He had no idea, but somehow the idea of living through the whole thing twice seemed worse. "Nah. Let's do it on camera. Get it over with."

"I was hoping you'd say that." Ollie made a note Shay couldn't make out in his notebook, his handwriting small and neat and nothing like Shay's rough scrawl. "No offence, but you don't seem like a man who can fake much."

"That a bad thing?"

"Not to me."

Another weighty silence settled over them. Shay craved the

moment of warmth they'd shared when their thighs had been pressed together. His entire body screamed at him to close the infinitesimal distance between him and Ollie, but he didn't have to.

Ollie moved first.

CHAPTER FIVE

OLLIE SANK into the vintage leather chair. The smell of books and parchment seeped into his soul, and for the first time in days, he felt grounded. The fear that his perspective would take a running jump out the back of the bus faded, and if he'd been alone, he might've laid his head on the table and slept.

But there was no time for a snatched nap. Tingling on the nape of his neck told him Shay was approaching, and for the next few hours, Ollie owed him his undivided attention.

Not that focusing on Shay was particularly hard. When Ollie hadn't been losing his mind on the road, Shay had occupied his every thought, and their library meeting had weighed heavily on his mind. At first, Shay hadn't seemed overly interested in the research Ollie was bringing to the table, but that changed when he learned Ollie had clues to his heritage he'd never allowed himself to wonder about before. They'd hardly spoken since the night of the Galway gig, but in the fleeting moments Ollie managed to gaze at him freely, Shay was clearly preoccupied.

He could be worrying about his girlfriend for all you know.

True, but from what Ollie had heard—and hunched over his laptop in the office, he'd heard a *lot*—Shay Maloney was single… lonely, even, and that was something Ollie understood all too well.

"You're such a thinker." Shay slid sinuously into the chair opposite Ollie. "Didn't your ma ever tell you if the wind changes, your face will stay like that?"

"What's wrong with my face?"

A beat of silence; then Shay averted his gaze, his fine features settling into an expression that was almost shy. "Nothing. Um… what are we doing here, then? Don't tell me I'm a Nordie. My nan wouldn't have liked that."

"If by nordie you mean Northern Irish, then no, I'm not about to tell you that. In fact, as far as I can tell you have no Irish blood in you at all."

Shay nodded slowly. "That shouldn't surprise me because if I didn't know it before, that name you gave me the other day definitely wasn't fucking Irish, but I almost feel like I've lost something."

"You didn't google your name?"

"Fuck no, I want to hear it from you."

He seemed to speak to himself as much as to Ollie, but the sentiment hung heavy in the air. Ollie took a deep breath and pointed at the camera he'd set up in the corner of the room. "Whenever you're ready, I'll turn the camera on, and we can start going through what I've set out to show you today, but there's still time to change your mind about learning everything on screen. We can run through it first… just you and me."

"You and me?" Shay's tongue darted out to lick his pillowy bottom lip. "You mean—"

"I mean off camera," Ollie cut in before his imagination started a goddamn rave.

"Off camera. Right." Shay sucked in a deep breath of his own. "I knew that."

It was on the tip of Ollie's tongue to ask what else he could've possibly meant, but Shay's obvious nerves kept him quiet.

He got up and checked the camera angle and fiddled with settings that were already perfect while Shay checked his blood sugar levels. "There's water on the table in the corner, and I've got snacks if you need them."

"Thought you weren't allowed to eat in libraries?"

"I won't tell if you don't."

Shay smirked and sat back in his seat. He kicked his boots off and tucked his long legs beneath him. "I should be fine, but I didn't get much sleep last night, so you might have to kick me a couple of times."

"Was it a late one, then? I thought Corina banished you all to bed at ten o'clock."

"She did, but she forgot to hand out the Valium, so I was counting sheep till dawn."

A shiver ran through Ollie. He'd been up most of the night too, torn between obsessing over today and fixating on the only part of Shay he'd been able to see—his twitching right foot. If he'd known he'd been awake too….

What? You'd have got up and gone over there? Crept into a space that's basically his bedroom like a fucking weirdo?

Jesus. Ollie shivered again. Shay Maloney was bad for his brain.

And he was staring at him, which was probably a sign Ollie needed to pull himself together. "Are you ready?"

Shay shrugged. "I guess so."

Ollie turned the camera on and slipped silently back to his seat. "I'll get up in a little while and do some panning shots while you look over what I've told you, but the first bit will be us talking."

"What about all the stuff you just said? That won't be in it, will it?"

"No. I'll edit that out. How about I kick you when we've started for real?"

That earned Ollie a grin he wasn't quite ready for. He scanned the table, checking for the dozenth time he had everything he needed, despite the fact that he'd laid it all out *hours* ago while the band had still been getting breakfast and taking turns in the tiny shower on-board the bus. *Fuck it.*

"Okay, we're going live in five, four, three, two, one." After a brief pause, Ollie kicked Shay under the table. The contact reminded him of the blissful ten minutes they'd spent in Galway with their legs pressed together, a silent storm of awkwardness and perfection that had only been shattered by an ambulance screaming past. A third shiver rocked Ollie's world, but for once, the professional buried deep within him won out.

He reclaimed his leg. "We're going to start in 1864, during the peak of the Danish-Prussian War to be exact. Have you ever heard of it?"

Shay leaned forwards. "Denmark and who?"

"Prussia," Ollie said. "In simple terms, it was a massive German state that covered a huge swathe of Northern Europe. Parts of Poland and Lithuania were included. Kaliningrad too. You'll find many definitions of what it meant to be Prussian, but the Nazis stopped using the term in 1934, and it was abolished entirely in 1947."

"After the Second World War?"

"Yes."

Ollie reached for the hefty book he'd come all the way to Belfast to study. He'd marked the page he needed with a teaspoon —the only thing he could find when he realised he was reluctant to risk losing his favourite pencil. *Freak*.

Shay plucked the spoon free and laughed. "Please tell me you haven't been crawling around the shelves sticking spoons in books?"

"I guess you'll find out soon enough." Ollie tapped the page. "Now pay attention."

Shay whistled. "Wow. You don't get that at the BBC."

"You don't get a lot of things at the BBC."

"You've worked there?"

"Once upon a time. Is this one of those moments when I need to kick you?"

Shay's expression sobered, and he regarded Ollie across the table, curiosity lighting up his gold-flecked eyes. "Do you have a story, Ollie?"

"I have lots of stories. They're all about you."

"What about yours?"

"That's not why we're here."

"Doesn't mean I don't want to hear it."

"Shay."

"What?"

Ollie cringed inwardly at the amount of editing he was going to have to do to make this piece viable if Shay carried on like this. He jabbed a finger at the camera. "Not now."

His clipped tone seemed to reach Shay. Something changed, and he snapped back to attention. "Sorry. Where were we?"

Ollie smoothed the page. "I was about to introduce you to your great-great-great-grandfather."

"My what?"

"Take a look." Ollie beckoned Shay forwards, realising too late that Shay's hair would flop forwards so close to his own face that he could smell his musky shampoo. "This man here"—he tapped the page—"is Rudolph Kaspersen."

"Kaspersen… that's, uh, Swedish, maybe?"

"Danish," Ollie corrected. "It means 'son of Kasper' if you take it literally, though God knows how far you'd have to go back to find the original Kasper, and by then, you might not be in Denmark at all."

"Danish." Shay studied the young man on the page. In full military gear, he was worlds apart from Shay. "Thank fuck for that. I thought you were going to tell me I was German."

"What's wrong with being German?"

"Nothing… to me, at least, but my nan would've hated that even more than me being a nordie. She was a bitter old crone."

"She sounds lovely."

"She was when she was baking. The rest of the time she had more bite than Chernobyl."

"*Anyway*," Ollie said. "Rudolph was a second lieutenant in the Danish army at the height of the war. In this picture, which was taken on the seventeenth of April, 1864, the day before the Battle of Dybbøl, he was eighteen years old."

"Eighteen? Wow. That's so young to be that rank." Shay traced the page with his fingertip. "I mean, it is now. Probably not in those days, right?"

"Right, and especially not in times of war—a war Denmark was losing. Leading up to the events at Dybbøl, the Prussians had laid siege to the Danes. For two months they bombarded them— the most intense bombardment in military history up until that point—then, on the eighteenth of April, 1864—"

"They attacked?"

"Yes, and the Danish forces were overrun very quickly, which was hardly surprising considering they were outnumbered four-to-one in most places."

Shay hunched over the book, probably obscuring his face from the camera. "What did that mean for him? For Rudolph?"

"Everything," Ollie said. "At the point when his position fell, the Prussians weren't taking prisoners. If the Danish troops had any chance of surviving, they had to fight their way out. Rudolph led what became a suicide attack on the Prussians. He fought bravely, and his brigade held up the Prussians for an hour or two, but by the end of the day, over half of them were dead."

"Did he make it out?" Shay's eyes were molten, his knuckles white as he gripped the edge of the desk. "Or was he killed in action?"

"He made it out." Ollie absorbed the sag of Shay's shoulders. "And that was the end of his military career. The Dybbøl offensive pretty much ended the war. The Danes signed a treaty on the thirtieth of October that year, and by then, Rudolph had already returned home."

"What happened next? For him, I mean. I don't care about the war."

"Not many people do," Ollie retorted. "That's why no one understands how Europe came to be the way it is, but I'll save that lecture for another day."

"You're a clever man."

"Not really. I just read books."

Shay leaned impossibly closer. "You don't *just* do anything."

Yet again, Shay had thrown a totally left-field statement at

Ollie and rendered him mute. Ollie opened his mouth. Shut it again.

Shay smirked. "I mean, could I have found all this shit online if I'd looked hard enough?"

Ollie snorted. Couldn't help it. "You won't find your soul on a computer, Shay."

"Right," Shay said. "And *that's* why you're a clever man."

It didn't make any sense, but Ollie was coming to accept that not much about the Shay Maloney he couldn't find in the history books did. The flesh and blood an inch away from him was complex—intricate—and perhaps Ollie could dig forever and never truly understand him. "Do you want to know what happened next or not?"

"I want to know."

"Rudolph went home and married a girl from his home town. They had a son and a daughter, and when the youngest was two years old, they emigrated to Scotland."

"Scotland?"

"Yes." Ollie made a mental note to remember Shay's tendency to respond to most of his statements with an incredulous one-word question. "We're going there next, I think? After your gigs here?"

Shay nodded, his gaze far away. "Something like that. I lose track when the bus is moving."

Lucky him. For Ollie, when the bus was in motion, every second seemed to last an hour, unlike now, when the two hours he'd set aside to film this segment were already almost up.

Ollie rose and attached the camera to a handheld gimbal. "There's more about Rudolph in that folder. Why don't you have a look through it while I pan around a bit?"

Shay nodded and drew the folder of papers towards him. Inside, among other things, he would find Rudolph's birth and death certificates, records of his marriage and subsequent children, and a single grainy photograph of the hardware shop that had remained in the Kaspersen family for a hundred years after the Battle of Dybbøl. Ollie had committed most pages to memory and leafed through them in his mind as he concentrated on capturing Shay's reactions.

Shay's gasp surprised him. "You didn't tell me about the others."

Ollie rounded the table, itching to put the camera down and peer over his shoulder, but instead positioned himself in Shay's line of sight and motioned for him to continue.

Shay shook his head slightly. "It says here that Rudolph's father and brothers were killed at Dybbøl. His uncle too. Out of five members of the Kasperson family who fought on that day, he was the only one to survive. Wow. That's crazy."

"It wasn't unusual in those days," Ollie said. "Think of the world wars when conscription was in place. Sometimes villages lost every man between eighteen and thirty-five."

"That doesn't make it right."

"No, it doesn't."

Ollie set the camera back on the tripod and returned to the table. Shay's hands were shaking. Ollie pressed their knees together. "Are you okay?"

"Yeah."

"Sure? It's a lot to take in when you're starting with nothing."

"I'm fine. Can I take some pictures of this stuff to show my dad?"

"Of course, but he can't share it on social media or anything. You need to keep it on the DL until the program comes out."

"You think my dad's on Facebook? He's barely accepted DVDs."

Ollie chuckled. "My dad is the same. Stuck in the eighties. It kinda works for my grandparents as they brought all the good bits from way before that, but my parents basically don't like spending money."

"Are you close to them?"

"Sometimes."

Shay tore his gaze from the papers spread out on the table. "Sounds loaded."

"Not on purpose." Ollie checked his watch. "We'd better wrap this up. I promised Corina I'd have you back by three."

Shay seemed reluctant to leave, still lost in all that the books and papers in front of him had revealed. Ollie wanted to let him stay, to open every relevant book in Belfast Library and give him the world he was missing, but they'd run out of time. Shay's story had begun a long time before Ollie received an email with his name in the subject line, and his current pages opened on a stage he was supposed to be soundchecking in twenty minutes' time.

Ollie turned the camera off and laid a cautious hand on Shay's slim shoulder. "I'm sorry, mate. We have to go."

Ten minutes later, they left the library. Shay insisted on carrying Ollie's laptop bag while Ollie shouldered the camera equipment.

"I thought you were joking when you said you'd be filming the whole thing on your own," Shay said.

Ollie shot him a sideways glance. "Even when I showed you examples from the last series?"

Shay shrugged. "To be honest, I wasn't really paying attention that day. I didn't understand how much it meant, you know?"

"I can imagine." Ollie had never been in Shay's position, so he could only gauge how he felt by assumption. "You did really well, though, if it's any consolation. It was like you forgot the camera was there, and that's the best way to be."

"I did forget," Shay said. "Even when you were moving around with it, it was like it was part of you."

A rueful snort escaped Ollie. "You should understand that. I don't make beautiful music, but I can't imagine ever being without the means to make a film. Even if it's a split-second clip on my phone, it's still part of me. I—"

He stopped. *What the fuck am I doing?* It was Shay who was supposed to be splayed open, not him. And Ollie didn't talk. Never had. His *babcia* said he had an imprisoned heart, and the right soul had the key. But his grandmother said a lot of things.

Shay nudged Ollie. Somehow, they'd both stopped walking. "I

understand," he said softly. "I just didn't see it in you straight away. I'm sorry."

"Sorry?" Ollie tilted his head. "What the fuck for?"

"For everything." Shay nudged Ollie again, his elbow lingering gently against Ollie's ribs. "My ma raised me to see people for who they are more than what they do. I didn't do that with you because my teeny brain had associated you with work more than being human. How fucked up is that?"

"Everything about doing what you love to make a living is fucked up."

"You think so?"

"No doubt." Ollie hated the cynicism lacing his words, but it was too late to take them back, and part of him didn't want to. Shay was living his best life with only a fraction of his identity tied to his soul, and Ollie was jealous. He pictured Shay on stage, his body moving in synch with the music *he'd created himself* and wanted to scream. *I want what he has.* But that would never happen, because he'd had it once, and it had burned away.

"Hey." Abruptly, Shay was right in front of Ollie, his lovely face so close Ollie could've kissed him if they were different people in different places. "I really am sorry. Sometimes how I feel about stuff doesn't make sense until I've written a song about it, and I'm not there yet with this whole... family thing. That shit makes me a weirdo."

He thinks he's the weirdo. It was endearing and horrifying all at the same time. Ollie wanted to touch him. Press their legs together, run his hand over his shoulder, up his neck and into his silky hair. Perhaps even hug him. But they were in the middle of Belfast with full hands. "You're not a weirdo, Shay. And how you see me doesn't matter."

Shay nodded and laid the laptop bag at Ollie's feet. "Fair enough."

He walked away.

CHAPTER SIX

DESPITE HAVING an all-access pass to the tour, Ollie didn't come to either of the Belfast shows. Shay didn't have to search the crowd for him. Somehow he just… knew.

The second show was sold out, the crowd packed into the traditional venue, drinking ale and stomping their feet. It was the gig of dreams—Shay's dreams, at least—but as he drew the show to a close on his penny whistle, a flat sensation stole over him. A mournful melody played out in his head, and he couldn't let it go.

A call for an encore went up. Larry offered Shay the cajon drum, but he shook his head. Smuggler's Beat never played the same show twice, and tonight—*right now*—he had to play something brand-fucking-new or his head would explode.

His bandmates had played with him long enough to know he was about to do something offbeat. They stepped quietly back but stayed close enough to join him if and when he signalled. He didn't know if he would. How could he when he didn't know what might come out until he lifted a harmonica to his lips.

The melancholic melody came back, but in the time that had passed between the end of the last song and the beginning of the next, it had grown a more tangible purpose. Shay often played the harmonica when he had no words to sing, just a feeling. He poured everything into it, and the single notes that came out said more than he ever could with his voice.

It was that way now. The melody was arching and painful and spoke of a grief Shay hadn't believed belonged to him. It spoke of the emptiness inside him he'd never recognised until this moment and the missing segments of his heart he felt guilty for wanting.

Shay faltered. Always the best at reading him onstage, Ben stepped forwards with his violin and picked up the tune, adding an Irish lilt that brought the crowd back to the party. Ben was clever like that, could read an audience in a way that Shay didn't even want to, and on nights like this, Ben was his lifeline.

The song evolved. Larry found a beat, and Jumbo wove a storming bass line into the roots of the melody. Mara picked up the melodeon, and the chain was complete. It was like having a jam session on a rollercoaster, but it worked for them. Improv had always been the heart behind Smuggler's Beat, and never more so than tonight.

They played out. The crowd roared. It was over.

And Shay left the stage as off-kilter as he'd arrived.

THE BUS was parked right outside the venue. In the morning, they'd leave to catch the ferry to Cairnryan in Scotland, but for now they were free to roam the streets of Belfast and celebrate the gig of the tour so far.

Shay trailed the others down a bustling street, poking at his phone as he stalked the venue's hashtag on Instagram to get some early reviews of the show. It wasn't something he often did, but tonight the sensation that he'd somehow fucked up wouldn't quit. Even when the posts he came across were all positive.

Ben dropped back from the group and draped an arm around Shay's shoulders. "You okay, superstar?"

Shay scowled. "Don't call me that."

"Why not? You smashed that encore tonight. We've got to nail that track down next time we're near a studio. It was *insane.* Where did it come from?"

Of course he would ask that. Ben wasn't much of a writer—he didn't have the patience—but he had an intuitive mind—a curious mind—and Shay usually had an answer for him. But not tonight. Though he'd shared the song with five thousand people, he didn't feel like dissecting the emotions that had put it there. At least not with Ben. "I don't know."

"Liar." Ben grinned. "Don't matter, though. Just let it do what you need it to do. Hey, are you hungry?"

That was another reason Shay adored Ben—his propensity to leave shit alone when he met a brick wall. And Shay *was* hungry. He'd eaten enough to stabilise his blood sugar for the show, but they hadn't had dinner yet. Perhaps that was why he didn't feel right.

If you say so.

Ollie's sardonic tone echoed in Shay's head, but despite his words being right on the money, Shay pushed them aside and slid an arm around Ben's waist. "I'm fucking starving. Can we get pizza?"

Ben grinned. "For you, superstar, anything. Ooh, I'll text Ollie. See if he fancies it."

He would've surprised Shay less if he'd punched him in the face. "You have his number?"

Engrossed in his phone, Ben didn't look up. "Yup. I got drunk with him yesterday."

"Did you? Where was I?"

"Sulking in your bunk with your notebook. You went straight back to the bus after the gig, remember?"

"Ollie wasn't at the gig."

Ben stopped walking and tapped his phone a few times before sliding it into his pocket. "No…," he said, clearly confused by Shay's needy reaction. "But he was smoking outside when we came out, sitting by the water all lonely and that, so I invited him for a pint. Turned into seven pints, obviously, but that's the Irish for you."

"He's not Irish."

"Nah, he's Polish, which means he can drink me under the table."

Shay didn't know what to say. Ben's apparent familiarity with Ollie burned him up inside, even though Ben was straight, and probably so was Ollie. Jealousy made Shay's stomach ache, and suddenly he wasn't hungry anymore.

Oblivious, Ben took Shay's arm again and hustled him forwards to catch up with the others. "There's an Italian place round the corner," he said. "Jog on, mate."

The Italian place turned out not to be Italian at all. It was owned by a couple of young hipsters who happened to make the best pizza Shay had ever tasted. "This is sacrilege," he said around a delicious mouthful. "We can't eat Irish pizza."

Mara flicked his ear. "Then don't. Leave some for the rest of us."

Shay ignored her and scarfed another slice. Despite feeling moody as fuck, his appetite had returned like a hungry bear as soon as they sat down, and now he couldn't stop eating, much to their amusement.

"We taking you back to the bus on a wheelbarrow again?" Larry said.

"Shopping trolley, more like," Shay retorted. "Can we get another of these sausage thin crusts?"

Larry rolled his eyes, but seeing as he absorbed Corina's role of mother whenever she wasn't around, he ordered more pizza.

A little while later, Shay was quite happily in a carb coma. It was so worth the manic insulin calculations he'd had to make to stop his blood sugar rising through the rooftops. He slouched back in his seat and sipped vodka and soda while the rest of the band got stuck in the beers. The restaurant had a bar below the balcony their table was on. It wasn't long before they lost Jumbo to a group of young women who'd piled in for cocktails.

Shay leaned on Larry and watched Jumbo work his magic. He was a tempestuous, lovable moron most of the time, but he oozed charm when he wanted to, and Shay wouldn't be surprised if he brought more than one guest back to the bus for the night.

As ever, Larry was too comfortable. Shay's eyes got heavier and heavier, and he was half-asleep when something Larry said to someone else made him jerk upright. "What?"

"Ollie." Larry jabbed his thumb over the balcony. "He's down there with Jumbo and Ben."

Shay looked out over the kicking bar below. While he'd been dozing, he'd missed a DJ setting up in the corner to play an eclectic mix of indie rock and deep house music, and also Ollie appearing in the crowd, which was unbelievable considering the thundering stampede of his heart now, the mad tingling at the back of his neck, and the flash of adrenaline that eclipsed any carb-induced sleepiness.

Ollie was wearing his standard leather-jacket-and-ripped-jeans combo, but he'd swapped his Vans for battered boots, and his jeans seemed tighter, hugging his compact frame in all the right places. Shay gulped more vodka as a flush of heat stole over his skin. Jesus. *Does he have to be so fucking fine?*

Shay felt Larry's shrewd gaze on him and wished there were more pizza left to hide behind. Or more vodka in his now-empty glass. *Fuck it.* "I'm going to the bar."

"'Bout fuckin' time," Larry muttered.

"Piss off." Shay gathered empty glasses. "I bought the last round."

"If you say so."

Shay couldn't take that phrase, even from Larry, without hearing Ollie's voice wrapped around every syllable. He drifted through the restaurant and down the ornate staircase, all the while wondering if his obsession with Ollie was terminal. If after the tour, when everyone had gone home, he'd be left shivering over random words some random dude from a TV company had once said to him.

Random dude. Shay shook his head. Goddamn, he needed another drink.

He deposited his stack of glasses on the bar and ordered a

double vodka and soda. It was his least favourite drink in the entire world, but with a belly full of pizza, it was the best of a bad bunch. He slurped half of it down in one long swallow, then scanned the bar. Recently, his gaze had seemed to land on Ollie without his trying, but he couldn't find him now. Jumbo was still there. Ben too. But Ollie was nowhere to be seen.

"Hey."

Shay jumped. Spun around like a part-time ballet dancer who should've stuck to the day job.

Ollie was right behind him, smirking, one gorgeous hand wrapped around a pint of something dark, the other with an unlit cigarette dangling from his fingers. "Sorry. Didn't mean to sneak up on you."

It was hard to hear him over the music. Shay stepped closer, leaning in. "What?"

"I said, sorry to sneak up on you. It's pretty loud in here."

Ollie's accent was thicker than usual, his speech slower. He was as drunk as Shay wanted to be, and God, if it didn't suit him. The pink tinge to his usually sharp eyes fit perfectly with the dark scruff on his jaw, and his softened features made him seem almost boyish. *I wonder how old he is.*

Asking seemed rude. So Shay didn't. He didn't say anything. Just stared until Ollie frowned and turned away.

Shit.

Shay grabbed Ollie's arm. "Sorry. I didn't mean to—"

Ollie wrenched his arm back before Shay could finish. "It's fine. I'll leave you to it."

He backed away before melting into the crowd like he'd never been there at all.

Anxiety built in Shay's gut, roiling with the heavy dinner and vodka he'd put away until he was sure he'd be sick. *I fucked up.* But how? What had he done that had spooked Ollie so badly? He replayed their brief encounter on a loop in his head, but the longer he stood alone in the packed bar, the less clear it became. *I need to find him.* Shay pictured the unlit cigarette in Ollie's hand, downed his drink, and ducked outside.

Ollie was on a bench by a war memorial, elbows on his knees, gazing at the ground as he smoked. Everything about him screamed to be left alone, but Shay was drunk and stupid and hurdled the back of the bench anyway.

He landed in a sitting position way too close to Ollie.

Oops.

Ollie didn't look up, just offered Shay a drag on his half-finished smoke.

Shay waved it away. "You're a clever man, and a weird one."

Ollie made a sound low in his throat. "If you say so."

"Don't be a dick."

"What do you want, Shay?"

Now there was a question. Shay leaned forwards, mirroring Ollie's pose. "I don't know."

Ollie nodded as if it made perfect sense. He flicked his cigarette butt into a nearby bin and stood. "Come for a walk?"

Lacking any brighter ideas, Shay stood too. There was frost on the ground. He stepped towards Ollie. His boot slipped on an icy patch and sent him lurching into Ollie.

Ollie caught him, his hands fire around Shay's wrists until he let go and slid an arm around Shay's waist. "Come on, you fucking hooligan. Let's go."

CHAPTER SEVEN

OLLIE HAD officially lost his mind. There was no other explanation as to why he was stumbling drunkenly through the centre of Belfast with his least messed-up arm clamped around Shay Maloney's sinful waist. It wasn't the beer. Couldn't be because he got drunk all the time and always wound up alone.

They meandered along a busy street until they turned a corner into a side road that was quieter. Shay didn't speak, and Ollie was glad of it. The chaos in his mind was loud enough without adding Shay's beautiful voice into the mix.

He thought about lighting another fag, but Shay didn't smoke. It hadn't seemed to matter before. For some reason, it did now.

"You didn't come to the gigs."

"Hmm?" Ollie glanced up to find Shay staring at him through a curtain of hair that had fallen into his face. "What?"

"The gigs," Shay repeated, biting his lip. "I thought you'd come."

Ollie looked away. "I wanted to, but—"

"But what?"

Ollie stopped walking. It was abrupt, and Shay lost his footing again. It was as easy as breathing to steady him once more and hard as hell to let him go.

So Ollie didn't let go. He kept his hands on Shay's arms,

rubbing them up and down to keep him warm through his thin denim jacket, all the while imagining the catastrophic inferno that would play out if Shay tried to touch him like that. "There's something about you," he whispered. "I can't spend all day around you, then all evening staring at you from a distance. I don't know why, I just… can't."

Shay swallowed. "You've never spent a whole day with me."

"Not literally. But trust me, my days right now are all about you."

"I don't understand."

"You will," Ollie said. "When we reach the end."

"That sounds like the end of the world. Again. Have we had this conversation before?"

"Maybe, but the middle might be different."

"Are you always so cryptic?"

Ollie sighed, regretting the uncertainty he'd forced into Shay's usually warm and welcoming smile. "Not on purpose. I've got a lot on my mind."

"Did I hurt you?"

"What?"

"When I grabbed you in the bar. You flinched."

"Did I?"

Shay moved impossibly closer. "Yes."

Ollie had no words. Just blood loaded with strong Belfast ale and a big hole in his brain from where he'd left his common sense on the bus. He kissed Shay, softly at first, but then like a starving man as Shay responded with a groan and a flick of his tongue.

He tasted of the lemon slice Ollie had seen in his drink at the bar. Of desire and friendship, and of everything Ollie couldn't have. But he couldn't stop. Kissing Shay was an illusion he could never shatter, and it went on and on until they ran out of air.

Ollie gasped in a breath, but Shay kissed him again before conscious thought returned. They staggered backwards. Ollie's back hit a cold brick wall, but even that wasn't enough to pull him to the surface, and for long, blissful minutes, he didn't care.

Kissing Shay was magic, and he didn't have the willpower to break the spell.

He spun them around, reversing their positions, and gripped Shay's face, deepening the kiss. A moan escaped him. Shay echoed the sound and slid his hands over Ollie's hips, hooking him closer as one leg rose up Ollie's body, pressing them together in ways Ollie couldn't describe.

God, I want him. But the thought alone was enough to remind Ollie that he couldn't have him for a million reasons beyond the path Shay's hands were blazing up his torso. *You're at work, dickhead. And he wouldn't want you anyway once you took your clothes off.*

Ollie had spent two long, hard years fighting to ignore the devil on his shoulder, but with Shay's flawless skin against his palms, he just… couldn't. Not tonight.

He kissed Shay one more time, then pulled away with Herculean effort and a soft sigh. "We should stop."

Shay blinked back at him. "Why?"

"Um… because this is a work thing for me, and I can't afford to fuck it up?"

He hadn't meant it as a question, but Shay's only answer was a slow nod, as though his own mind was in a million pieces too. "I wouldn't tell anyone."

"Neither would I, but that's not really my point."

Perhaps sober Shay would've pushed him, but this version of him seemed as lost as Ollie felt. Unable to resist a last jolt of sensation, Ollie kissed the very tip of his nose. "You want me to walk you back to the bar?"

"Nah." Shay rubbed his hands over his face. "I think… I think I want to sleep."

Ollie folded his arms tight around himself. "Come on, then. I'll take you back to the bus."

Shay slept the entire journey from Belfast to Edinburgh. Ollie knew this because he checked every six seconds to see if he was awake yet.

The rest of the band checked on him too. On the ferry crossing, Larry came past and tucked another blanket over him. At Inverness, Mara bent over his bunk and did something Ollie couldn't see.

At a service station, Ollie fled the bus to catch a smoke to calm his nerves. Being hung-over and dog-tired had distracted him from being on the road, but as his head cleared, it found new ways to kill him.

Ben joined him in the smoking shelter.

"It's nice," Ollie said. "That you all look after Shay."

"We all look after each other in this band, mate."

"That's nice too."

Ben chuckled. "Shay does make it easy, though. I mean, the last band I was in, we were like brothers, man, but this lot were wild when we first started out. Took me and Larry a while to help them see life on the road was far easier if we took care of each other. Just so happens Shay needs it more than the rest of us sometimes."

Ollie liked Ben. The fiddle player always seemed to know—and say—exactly what people needed to hear. No padding or bullshit. "Is he okay?"

"Shay? Yeah, course he is. Kid's tired, that's all. He leaves his heart on the stage, and it takes it out of him when he's got no proper bed to go home to. He'll be right as rain by this afternoon."

Ollie believed him because he had to. Ben knew Shay—and life on the road—far better than Ollie, but guilt that he might've upset Shay gnawed at him. And then came scathing self-loathing. Shay had played two packed-out shows in a row, on top of media commitments, and working with Ollie. Add in a hangover, and it wasn't hard to see why he'd slept the day away. *He probably doesn't even remember last night.*

But even as Ollie thought it, he knew it wasn't true. *Ollie* had been off his nut last night, and he recalled every millisecond of Shay's lips on him. His taste, his smell. His hands ghosting where

Ollie wanted them most but in the same breath couldn't bear them to be.

He'll remember.

The certainty stayed with him through two piggybacked cigarettes and carried him back to the bus, but when he boarded to find Shay not only awake, but up, dressed, and picking idly at his favourite guitar, the bland smile that greeted him chased the feeling away.

It was the same smile Shay had given him the day they'd met. The same smile he gave anyone who didn't truly hold his attention. Whether he remembered last night or not, perhaps Shay had made a conscious decision to forget.

OLLIE WOKE with a jump. Instantly, silence surrounded him, making the pounding of his pulse even louder. *Fuck.* He sat up and pressed a hand over his chest. His thumping heart wasn't as fast as it sounded in his head—it never was—but disquiet crawled under his skin all the same.

Pushing the books he'd fallen asleep with off his torso, he absorbed the claustrophobic box that was his makeshift bedroom. Despite it being the middle of the day, he was cloaked in darkness. The blackout curtain had been pulled around his bunk—by whom, he had no idea.

Embarrassment joined the creeping sensation in his veins. He hadn't meant to knock out, but ten days of living on his nerves had finally caught up with him. When the band had left for their Edinburgh gig the night before, he'd settled on his bunk to finalise the information he planned to reveal to Shay in Glasgow. Last time he'd checked his watch, it had been a little after midnight. Now it was ten o'clock in the morning, and drawing the curtain open confirmed that he'd missed the band coming and going.

He was alone.

Relief and disappointment fought for dominance. Ollie had hardly set eyes on Shay since their drunken fumble in Belfast, but the growing anxiety in his bones made him crave solitude, a limiting habit he'd never tried that hard to kick. He missed the bustle and noise of the band bickering over breakfast. But he didn't miss curious eyes on him—Shay's curious eyes.

Loser.

Fuck it.

I don't care.

For a long moment, he almost believed it, but then the bus door opened and the band piled in: Larry, Mara, Jumbo, and Ben. Shay was last, head bowed, scribbling in a notebook. He didn't look up as he shuffled down the aisle and flopped on his bed, and the lack of eye contact—of any contact—flayed Ollie. *What do you expect? You snogged him, then shoved him away.*

But so what if he had? They were both adults. There was no need for Shay to blank him.

Irritation flooded Ollie, an emotion that often got the better of him, especially when he knew it was irrational. Shay hadn't been around to blank him, and before they'd messed around, there'd been plenty of occasions when Shay had been too engrossed in his work to notice *anyone*, let alone Ollie, some knobber from a TV company who blew hot and cold like fucking whiplash.

The bus engine rumbled to life. Alarmed, Ollie threw his legs over the side of the bed and planted his feet on the floor. The band was due in Glasgow that evening, but sleeping in had left Ollie no time to ground himself enough to face even the briefest of road journeys.

Fuck this.

He stamped into his Vans, grabbed his camera bag, thankful he'd slept in his clothes, and made it to the front of the bus a split second before the driver took the handbrake off.

"Wait up, mate. I'm getting off here."

CHAPTER EIGHT

____

"HE DID say he wasn't going to be here for the whole tour." Corina kept her gaze on her ever-present iPad. "I've only got the dates and times he's booked you for filming in the schedule. Where he is the rest of the time isn't my concern."

Shay glowered. He'd asked the question as casually as he could, putting it to Smugs, the bus driver, first and then gradually working his way up to Corina. After an afternoon of dead ends, he'd counted on her having an answer for him. And also on her not giving a witch's tit why he was asking, which she clearly didn't.

Swallowing a growl of frustration, Shay stomped out of the side room Corina had commandeered as an office for the next few days. He'd fed her a bullshit reason for wanting to know Ollie's whereabouts, but the truth was, he couldn't get Ollie's abrupt departure from the tour out of his head—Ollie's tense shoulders and set jaw, his wide, anxious eyes, and the scent of… fear as he'd rushed past Shay's bunk in his hurry to get off the bus.

Your imagination is fucking nuts. Truth. It always had been. But Ollie had jumped off the bus for a reason, and Shay would've bet his oldest banjo that it wasn't a pleasant one.

He made his way back to the rehearsal room. Most of the band were huddled in corners, tuning up or tapping out lazy rhythms.

Only Ben didn't appear occupied with gig preparation and instead sat hunched over his phone.

Shay cuffed his shoulder on his way past. "Leave that girl alone. You were up all night FaceTiming her."

Ben grunted. "Fuck off. Not my fault she lives in New Zealand, is it?"

"Ain't it?" Jumbo called. "She moved back *after* you hooked up with her."

Ben's glare would've burned Jumbo alive if he hadn't possessed such a kind face. As it was, Jumbo just laughed, and Ben turned back to Shay. "Anyway. I'm not even talking to Eve. I'm talking to Ollie."

"Ollie? Why? Where is he?"

If Ben was surprised by the influx of Ollie-themed questions, it didn't show. He shrugged and held up his phone. "He's in Glasgow."

"He's here?"

"Well, no. He ain't *here*, knobhead. But he's in the city. Reckons he'll link up with us tomorrow."

"But—" Shay stopped. Swallowed down a mouthful of questions and tried not to scrutinise Ben's phone screen. He should've been relieved. Ollie was close by, and he'd be back on the tour by tomorrow, but Shay couldn't silence the whisper in his head that something wasn't quite right. "Um… can I have his number?"

"What for?"

"What do you care?"

"I don't." Ben grinned. "I just like watching you squirm. What's going on with you two? Someone only has to mention him and you get all giddy and shit."

"Piss off and give me his number."

Shay had a better mean mug than Ben. After a fleeting stand-off, Ben buckled and sent Ollie's contact card to Shay's phone.

Ignoring the chuckles that followed him, Shay left the room again, retreating to a quiet corner of the big venue to save Ollie's number in his phone and then stare at a blank WhatsApp message for the rest of the afternoon. Because really, what was he supposed to say? *Please come back. I'm freaking out thinking you left because I snogged you?*

Because Ollie's world was all about Shay.

Idiot.

OLLIE: *MEET me at the University of Glasgow Library, tomorrow, 11 am —Ollie*

Shay stared at the message, wondering if he was still asleep. He'd floated off stage last night and climbed straight into bed, and despite ten hours sleep and a decent breakfast, he still didn't feel quite awake yet.

Dreaming of Ollie messaging him didn't seem all that bad, but the notion that Ollie had somehow procured Shay's phone number was somehow better, even if it was clearly for work purposes.

Shay's fingers hovered over the screen as he debated his response. Playing the packed-out Glasgow venue had blown some of the worry webs from his mind, but he still wanted to know where Ollie had been. And *why*. Fuck it. He wanted to know everything about Ollie that Ollie would deign to tell him, and he didn't understand it. One kiss and he was obsessed?

Bullshit. You were obsessed before.

Shay groaned and dropped his phone on the table. Corina glanced up from her work. "Everything okay? Do you need more food?"

"I'm fine," Shay snapped, then regretted it. "Sorry, I mean, no, thanks. I'm good."

Corina laughed. "You're so sweet when you're grumpy."

"I'm not grumpy."

"No? Because the alternative is you're simply a wanker, Shay, and I'm pretty sure that's not true. Do you want to take a seat and talk to me?"

Shay chewed on his lip. Corina was a manager—business always came first—but beneath the lists and schedules, the rules and limits, she did care. Would she understand that Shay had developed a monstrous crush on a TV researcher she'd likely been reluctant to let on the tour in the first place? Probably not, but that didn't mean Shay couldn't pick her brain.

He flopped into a hard plastic chair. "I like someone."

Amusement flickered in Corina's serious gaze. "Is this the part where I have to remind you that you signed a contract with the record company promising not to produce vile headlines for the tabloids?"

Shay rolled his eyes. "Do you have to ask that? You know I don't shag around."

It was true. Shay could pull a different face every night if he wanted to, but he didn't. Casual sex was Jumbo's jam, not his.

"So what's the problem?" Corina said. "Have you met someone who doesn't like you being on tour?"

"It's not that." Though maybe *Ollie* had a girlfriend who was missing him. Huh. Shay hadn't thought of that. *Fuck. What if he's married?* Shit like that had put him off hooking up with blokes in the first place. *Goddammit.* Shay sighed. "Stuff it. Never mind."

Corina studied him over the rim of her cool AF red-framed glasses. "Fair enough, but I'm going to say one thing to you, Shay, and that's don't let what's going on in your professional life keep you from having a personal life that means something. You're a young man now, but one day you're going to wake up and be a forty-year-old spinster, married to nothing but your job, and trust me, it's not fun."

"I wasn't saying I wanted to get married. Blimey."

Corina laughed. "Good. You're too busy for that nonsense right now."

"Is that your way of giving me the most mixed message ever?"

"Of course," Corina said. "I'm not your mother. And seriously… you're coming to me for romantic advice? I can't even figure out how Tinder works."

The conversation was going nowhere Shay wanted to be. Corina was a beautiful, intelligent woman, and he'd drunkenly told her a million times to put her iPad down and find someone who'd tell her so every damn day. But they'd reached the point in their unique bond of friendship where she'd probably deck him if he told her again. Instead, he took a chance. "How much do you know about Ollie?"

Corina's expression didn't change. If she'd figured out why he was asking, it didn't show. "A bit. I checked him out before I approved him joining the tour."

"Why didn't I get to check him out too?"

"Because you had other things going on. Why? Is there a problem?"

"No! No… uh… not at all. I just wondered about him, that's all."

Corina stared at him, a tiny crease crinkling her brow. "Listen, I know I gave you a hard time about this project, but if it's stressing you out, there's probably *something* I can do to get it canned. I'd probably have to use your diabetes as an excuse, but—"

"Jesus-fucking-Christ." Shay banged his head on the table. "Just forget it, okay? Forget this entire conversation."

He started to stand up. Corina grabbed his arm and yanked him back down. "All right, all right. Calm your tits. You want to know about Ollie? Fine. I'll tell you everything I know."

Walk away, walk away. But the temptation was too strong. Shay sat down again. Leaned forwards and dropped his elbows on the table. "I'm listening."

SHAY STOOD in the shadows across the road from the library, watching as Ollie approached from the opposite end of the street. He had his hood up, hiding from the drizzly Scottish rain, but Shay saw enough of his face to make his heart stutter. *I've missed him. How is that even possible?*

But it was true. Ollie's presence on tour had been unobtrusive and quiet, but since that very first day, Shay had instinctively sought him out. Wherever they were, whatever they were doing, in his peripheral vision he'd always seen Ollie. The last twenty-four hours had been strange, though. To see him properly, he'd had to close his eyes, but he'd stopped doing that once he'd heard what Corina had to say.

"I already knew his name. Five years ago, he was the hottest young filmmaker out there. He won every independent award going, and word was he was about to make this real hard-hitting documentary about the migrant camps in Calais. He had a rep for pulling no punches, and the world was waiting, but…."

"But what?" Shay said.

Corina shrugged. "It never came to light. Something happened to drop him off the map for a couple of years, and the next thing I knew, he was popping up in my inbox as a researcher for Sky. I'm guessing something happened in his personal life, but I didn't dig too hard. Given that I've never heard a bad word about him, it didn't seem right."

Shay couldn't decide how he felt about what Corina had told him. Part of him was relieved that he knew *something* about Ollie, but the rest of him was consumed with guilt. Ollie didn't owe him anything. They hardly knew each other.

Ollie disappeared into the library. Shay debated letting him go, sacking the whole project off and returning to a life he understood—music and friendship. But his feet had other ideas, and he was halfway across the road before a conscious decision to follow Ollie caught up with him.

Inside, the library was huge and smelled exactly the same as the library in Belfast had—of dust and paper. Of knowledge and wisdom. It was a scent Shay had come to associate with Ollie, though all he'd smelled on Ollie when he'd been close enough to breathe him in had been beer, fags, and desire.

Shay shivered. *Stop. It was one fucking kiss.*

"Shay?"

He spun around. As usual, Ollie was right behind him, eyeing him as though he couldn't decide if Shay was an irritation or an unexploded bomb.

"I got you a pass," Ollie said. "We'll only be here a few hours, but it's valid until tomorrow."

"Uh, thanks?"

Ollie grinned a little. "What? No plans to ditch the postgig piss-up and chill out with the books?"

It was as though nothing had changed. As though the mad, frantic kisses they'd shared in Belfast had never happened. As though Ollie hadn't been MIA for twenty-four hours and Shay hadn't spent the entire time driving himself fucking insane wondering why.

Shay searched for words. Found none.

Ollie shook his head slightly and pointed up. "Come on. We need to go upstairs."

They rode the lift to the eighth floor. Shay trailed Ollie while he selected some books; then they climbed the stairs to the highest level. Ollie had the key to a private room. It was smaller than the one in Belfast, with no windows and two chairs packed tightly around a compact table. There was no room for the stack of books Ollie had carried up four flights of stairs.

He didn't seem to mind. He set the books on the floor and his laptop on the table, instantly engrossed as it flashed to life.

Shay hovered in the doorway, shifting his weight from one foot to the other and back again. Ollie was sexy as hell when he let his inner nerd out to play, but Shay was trying not to notice. Stepping closer—claiming a seat at the table—seemed like taking the pin out of the grenade.

"Are you going to stand there all day?" Ollie glanced up. "Because if you're in a hurry, it won't help to get started late."

"I'm not in a hurry."

"Come and sit down, then. I've got something for you to look at while I set the camera up."

Shay admitted defeat and crossed the room in one long stride. He sat at the table, holding his breath so Ollie would seem farther away. On the laptop screen was a black-and-white pencil sketch of a woman with long curly hair. It was dated 1694.

"Who's that?"

Ollie adjusted the height of his tripod and pressed a few buttons on the camera. Then he came back to the table and slid into the other chair. "You want to know now or after I count us in?"

Shay rolled his eyes. "Just get on with it."

"Wow. You're in a mood."

"And you're a dick. Can we just get this done?"

Ollie blinked. For a moment his slate gaze was wide and confused. Then something settled in it, and he shrugged. "Whatever. Going live in five, four, three, two, one."

"Who's that?" Shay asked again.

"Her name was Anna," Ollie said. "She was briefly married to your sixth great-grandfather."

"Sixth great-grandfather? What does that even mean?"

"Exactly what it says. He was three generations before Rudolph, if that helps, but on the other side of your family tree. From your father's side."

Shay sucked in a breath. "So the Danish stuff comes from my mother? I never thought to ask the other day."

"It was a lot to take in." Ollie shifted. In Shay's imagination he moved closer, but he couldn't be sure. "But yes. The Danish blood comes from the maternal side. Anna was Lithuanian."

"Lithuania? That was part of Prussia, right?"

"It's complicated, but the region where I found records for Anna would certainly have been considered Prussian at some point."

"Wow. So I had family on both sides of the war?"

Ollie nodded. "It's likely."

Shay studied the picture again. The woman had an angular face and wore tatty clothes. "She looks wild. Tell me about her?"

"Wild would probably be a good way to describe her." Ollie reached for one of his magic books and set it carefully on the small table. "I think you'll like her, though. After last time, I figured you needed to see something—or someone—that resonated more with your own life."

"I felt something for Rudolph."

"I know you did."

Shay swallowed. *How did you know?* But he didn't say it.

Couldn't. Because asking the question would force Ollie to answer, and Shay wasn't sure he could handle whatever he had to say. "What kind of person was she? She doesn't come off rich or noble."

A beat of silence. Then Ollie dragged his gaze back to the book. "She wasn't, but she did rub shoulders with Lithuanian nobility, especially when she was younger. She was an accomplished musician—she played all kinds of instruments, like you."

"Seriously?"

Like magic, the weirdness cloaking the room faded away. Ollie spun the book so Shay could see it. "Seriously. At eighteen, she was the principal lutist for the royal court, unheard of for a peasant girl. I haven't managed to find out how she was able to learn so many instruments as a child, but she had an uncle who had some kind of craft. It might've been that he made instruments for the nobility and she spent her childhood around him."

"That's mad," Shay whispered. "What happened to her?"

"*Lots* of things. At some point, she left the royal court, possibly to marry, but there's a gap after that of around ten years. The next records I found have her roaming the countryside, playing folk music in religious sects on all kinds of instruments." Ollie flipped a page. "I don't even know what some of them are called."

Shay stared at the series of photographs spread over the double page. "She smoked a pipe?"

Ollie laughed. "Yes…. Anna was a rebel. A free thinker, I suppose you could call her. Eventually, she broke away from religion too and roamed around on her own, playing in villages she happened across, writing poetry, though I haven't found any of that. I do have a recording of the style of music she might've played, if you want to hear it?"

"Fuck yeah."

Ollie shot Shay a look that made his toes feel strange. "I thought you might say that."

Shay's boots suddenly seemed too tight. He thought he'd steeled himself enough to spend the day with Ollie, but somehow he'd forgotten how intense Ollie was. How a single glance could make it seem as though Ollie could see not only how he felt in that moment, but every emotion that had ever crossed his heart.

The tingling in Shay's feet spread. He watched Ollie tap at his phone and then set it close to Shay. On the screen, Shay recognised the Spotify logo, but everything else was in another language. "What's the song called?"

"It doesn't have a name," Ollie said. "It was recorded by some Lithuanian students in the seventies from some parchments in the National Museum."

A deep stringed bass cut off any reply Shay might have made. It throbbed and rose in volume until it was joined by a chanting vocal—layered female voices that left goosebumps on Shay's skin. It was haunting and beautiful and nothing like he'd imagined.

When it was over, he let out a long breath. "Wow. I thought it would be more… fuck, I don't know. Simple, maybe? Rougher? That was so delicate."

Ollie nodded. "I know what you mean. Lithuania was Christianised in the thirteen hundreds, so traditional music became heavily influenced by Gregorian chants. There was a lot of opera around the royal court too, but that may have been what Anna ran away from."

Shay couldn't tell if Ollie was joking, but the theory resonated with him. "I quit my classical music degree to play the banjo in workingmen's clubs."

"It's in the blood, then."'

"But how? Anna's connection to me is through marriage."

"Yes, but she had a child when she was married to your sixth great-grandfather. She left the baby in the capital—your fifth great-grandmother, also called Anna—so her blood remained in your family even though they never saw her again."

"When did she die?"

"I don't know. Her trail went cold, and I've tried everything to pick it up over the last few days because I figured you'd want to know more, but all I could find was a folk band in Vilnius who still play music from the region where Anna was most well known."

The idea that Ollie had spent the last few days still searching for Anna nearly finished Shay off. He rubbed his chest, trying to ease the knot there. Discovering Anna had left him breathless—awed in a way he couldn't describe. Was it wrong to wish it had come from someone else? To resent Ollie for having the keys to his past when he had zero interest in Shay's present?

He sighed again, avoiding Ollie's gaze. "Do you have a recording of the folk band?"

"No, but I have a YouTube link I can send you."

"That works."

Ollie handed Shay his phone. Shay lifted the link and sent it to himself on WhatsApp without much conscious thought, but a flutter tickled his chest when his own phone buzzed. *It's professional, you goon.* But to Shay it meant something, even if it meant nothing.

CHAPTER NINE

"This was Rudolph's shop?" Shay stood in front of the Italian cafe, staring up at the grand old building. "Where he sold hardware?"

"That's right. It was in business until the sixties, when this family took it over."

"What happened to Rudolph after that?"

Ollie panned the camera around Shay in a sweeping shot, grateful these streets weren't as busy as the ones around the library. "Not much. He died not long after his son took over the shop, and his daughter moved to England. I don't think he ever got over what happened in the war, though. Lots of Danish people didn't."

Shay was silent, like he had been for long periods since they'd left the library. Ollie's presence seemed to irritate him, but he'd jumped at the opportunity to take a detour on the way back to the bus, his curiosity about his past apparently too strong to ignore.

Ollie was trying not to notice how gorgeous he was standing stock-still on the pavement, framed by the afternoon sun. And trying not to admit how awkward their encounter had been so far. He'd left the tour to clear the air—among other reasons—but his vibe with Shay was heavier than ever. Suffocating, and yet too thrilling to push aside. *Man, this dude fucks me up.*

And viewing him on the tiny camera screen was pure torture. Ollie shut the camera off. Shay didn't seem to notice, even when Ollie closed the distance between them, resisting the urge to nudge him like he might've done a week ago. "That's it for the day, unless there's anything else you want to know?"

"Know about what?"

Shay still wasn't looking at him. Frustration rippled through Ollie, and though he knew he deserved Shay's indifference, he wanted to shake him all the same. "About... Rudolph, Anna, what we're gonna do next."

"I thought it was a big mystery."

"That doesn't mean I won't tell you anything."

"No?" Shay finally turned. The sun was still behind him, its shadow obscuring his face. "Then why won't you tell me what's bothering you so much?"

"Bothering me?"

Shay rolled his eyes. "Don't deflect. Just tell me to fuck off. It's easier... and quicker."

"I don't want you to fuck off."

"Then what *do* you want?" Shay stepped forwards, breaking free of the sun as he invaded Ollie's personal space—all milky skin, long limbs, and a gaze so fierce it pinned Ollie in place. "Because this shit between us is fucking weird."

Ollie swallowed. He couldn't deny it. He'd messed around with people on the job before and had always been able to push it aside when it mattered. To put his desire in a box and leave it there. But that had been before... *that*, and before Shay. *Fuck this.* "Are you hungry?"

THEY GOT tiny mugs of espresso and an Italian all-day breakfast each. Ollie hadn't eaten properly in days. He figured he wasn't hungry, but the sight of the heaping plate proved him wrong.

He watched Shay check his blood sugar and inject himself with an insulin pen. "Does that hurt?"

Shay shrugged. "I don't know. It's my normal, so I don't really notice, but I suppose it must do. Getting blood from my fingers bothers me more, though. They get sore from playing guitar anyway."

"Did you play guitar at university?"

"What? For the week I was there?" Shay let his T-shirt drop, robbing Ollie of his pale abdomen. "A bit, but it was the flute that got me into Goldsmiths."

"Goldsmiths?"

"Yup. I scored a scholarship, then ditched it. My parents were so proud… not."

"I bet they're proud now." Ollie spoke without thinking and winced. "Sorry… I mean, I bet your mum was proud of you."

Shay reached for a slice of olive-oil-soaked toasted ciabatta. "She was. Eventually. I broke her heart to begin with, though. Working class Derby boy smashing it in London, prestigious orchestras and all that…. She loved that shit."

Ollie tried to picture Shay in smart clothes, toeing the line in a classical orchestra. Couldn't. It just didn't fit. "Any regrets?"

"Never. Life's too short."

Clichéd quotes got on Ollie's nerves, but there was nothing cliché about Shay. He waited for Shay to start eating, then followed suit, inhaling half his food before he raised his eyes to find Shay watching him. "What?"

"Nothing. Just never seen you eat before. I was starting to think you ran on coffee and fags alone."

He was more right than Ollie cared to admit. "You forgot beer. And rum. I like a bit of that."

"I've seen you drink."

Of course he had. Ollie's lips burned as though the kisses they'd shared had happened moments ago, not days. His leg shifted instinctively to find Shay's under the table, and he caught it at the last second.

He ate more food, but the crispy prosciutto and roasted tomatoes were heavy in his stomach, and his espresso cup was empty. "I'm sorry about that."

"About what?"

"About snogging you when I knew better."

"Better than what?" Shay set his elbows on the table and leaned forwards. "We're both adults."

"I know, but this job is important to me. And look how messed-up things already are."

"You don't think they'd be better if we let shit happen?"

Ollie poked at a chilli-laced fried egg. It did nothing to stop him falling down the vortex of Shay's molten gaze. "We can't do that."

"Why not? I mean, I'm not trying to persuade you to fancy me, but I don't want things to be weird between us. I like you, Ollie. Even if you are a bit of a dick."

A hysterical chuckle escaped Ollie. "You can't just tell me you like me and leave it at that."

"What can I say? The truth falls out of me—can't fucking help it." Shay dropped his gaze and returned to his food.

Guilt warred with engrained bad habits, and Ollie's heart beat too fast. Too loud. Too hard. He couldn't breathe.

He pushed his plate away. "You asked what was bothering me… like you knew it was something outside of the mess we've made here."

"Uh-huh." Shay didn't look up. "You left the bus like a rat in a fire. I was scared you wouldn't come back."

Like a rat in a fire. Nausea washed over Ollie. "I came back," he whispered.

Shay put his fork down and reached across the table. His fingers felt like lava as they wrapped around Ollie's. "But why did you run?"

THEY DITCHED the cafe and took a walk through a nearby park. Shay had let go of Ollie's hand when they left, but he stayed close, and their elbows bumped as they strolled through the trees.

Ollie latched on to the sensation of Shay brushing against him.

Used it to tie himself down to the world. "I don't like talking about myself."

"No shit. You've been with us for two weeks, and no one knows squat about you."

"Two weeks? Is that all? Feels like a year."

"Because you hate it?"

"I don't hate it."

"I don't believe you. The only time you seem happy is when you've got your nose in a book."

Ollie laughed, and it sounded like it was someone else. "How is that any different to you with your music? I'm a nerd, bro. It's who I am."

Shay stopped walking. "It's not all you are, though."

"Maybe it should be."

"Why?"

"I don't know?"

"That shouldn't make sense, but it does." Shay took Ollie's hands and squeezed them, once, before letting them go and resuming his aimless amble.

Ollie trailed after him and reclaimed his place pressed up against Shay's side, even closer than they'd been before. "It makes too much sense to me sometimes. I have to limit how much work I take on, or I'd never stop."

"But it doesn't make you happy."

It didn't seem to be a question, but Ollie shook his head anyway. "It keeps me calm, but, no… it doesn't make me happy."

"What does?"

"You think I know?"

"You must do, unless you've never been happy, Ollie."

Ollie thought hard. An article he'd read once, written by an American soldier, flashed into his mind. The soldier's heart had stopped beating, and as he'd neared death, an errant thought had pulled him clear. *I can't die. I've never been happy.* The quote had stuck with Ollie, though he hadn't known why—perhaps until now. "I thought I was happy once, but I was just young. Innocent, maybe. It was a long time ago."

"You think you can't get it back?"

"You can't take back innocence, Shay. When it's gone, it's gone."

"Mate, you have a maudlin mind."

"That your way of calling me a miserable bastard?"

Shay stared hard at something in the distance. "Not at all. You want to sit?"

"Hmm?"

"The venue is just up there, but I'm not ready to go back yet." Shay pointed at a nearby bench. "Sit with me, Ollie? Please?"

As if Ollie could refuse. As if he wanted to. Or perhaps he did, but the pull to be with Shay was somehow stronger than the vice around his heart.

He sat on the bench and lit a cigarette he didn't really want. Watching it burn gave him something to do, but he didn't smoke it. Just waited… for Shay, or for something else. Who the hell knew?

Shay sat beside him, close but not close enough. "I did a thing."

"A thing?"

"Yeah." Shay twisted on the bench to face him. "When you left the other day, I asked Corina some questions about you."

"What kind of questions?"

Shay bit his lip. "The nosy kind. I'm sorry."

Ollie leaned forwards and away from Shay, gaze fixed on the ground, and took a deep drag on his half-burned cigarette. "What did she tell you?"

"Not much. Just that you were some BBC hotshot before you were MIA for a few years. She didn't know any details, and I'm glad of it—I felt super guilty afterwards, like I'd plundered your confidence or some shit."

"You did." Ollie's tone was flat. No anger or rebuke, merely cold fact. "What difference does my life up until this point make to yours?"

"If I knew that, I'd have either asked you or not asked at all."

Ollie sighed. Shay hadn't been joking when he'd said he didn't often make sense about emotions he hadn't put to music yet. "You could've asked me."

"Would you have answered?"

"Probably not, but that's my prerogative. Why do you need to know my life story?"

Anyone else might've matched Ollie's sharp tone. Defended themselves with the belligerence Ollie perhaps deserved. Shay slipped his arm around Ollie's tense shoulders and said nothing for a long moment before he hummed a low tune Ollie recognised, though he couldn't put a name to it.

"I suppose it's because you know mine," Shay said softly when his tune had played out. "You know so much about me—more than I know myself—and I know nothing about you except that you kiss like a fucking demon… and you hate being on tour with me. With us."

"I don't hate being on tour—"

"Yes, you do," Shay snapped. "You think I can't see how miserable you are? That I don't notice when you duck out at mealtimes and stay up all night with your laptop? That you can't wait to get off the bus and away from me—from *us*—whenever we stop?"

Ollie laughed. "You think I'm trying to get away from *you*? That everything you've seen in me only manifested itself *two weeks* ago? Mate, you're either arrogant as fuck or tapped in the head."

"Which do you think it is?"

"Both. Neither. I don't fucking know." Ollie flicked his cigarette away with less care than he usually would. He scrubbed his hands down his face. He hadn't cried in years, but the weight of Shay's gaze on him scratched a wound that made his eyes sting. "Look, I'm not some international man of mystery, I'm just messed-up, okay? It's got nothing to do with you or the tour. I'm like this at home."

"Where is home?"

"Stanmore. It's a few miles north of—"

"I know where it is."

Ollie's hands started to shake. He let them drop from his face and folded his arms. Shay tugged on his elbow, his fingers slipping too far up Ollie's arm until Ollie flinched and yanked it free. He didn't look at Shay. "I don't like being on the road. I mean, like, literally on the road. I'm okay if I'm driving, but I'm a shit passenger."

Shay shifted on the bench. Ollie couldn't tell if he'd moved closer until his arm began to throb again, as though Shay's hand was hovering over it. "You get carsick?"

Ollie snorted. "No, Shay. I don't get carsick. It's more like a phobia, I guess, like a fear of flying, though I'm not sure what I'm actually afraid of anymore, and I can get on a plane just fine."

"Have you had it a long time?"

"No."

Ollie braced himself for the next question, but it never came. Shay leaned forwards and mirrored Ollie's pose, hunched shoulders, elbows on his knees. Another silence settled over them, but it was lighter this time, as though Shay had lifted a shadow from Ollie's mind.

The quiet was soothing to Ollie's scratchy soul, but the urge to fill it with something—anything—to acknowledge Shay was too strong to ignore.

His hands were still trembling. He ignored the tremors and reached for one of Shay's hands, twining their fingers together before he could change his mind. "I've never told anyone that."

Shay dragged his gaze from the ground. It was alive with emotions Ollie couldn't quite decipher. "Why did you tell me?"

I wanted you to know. "You asked."

"No one's ever asked you about it before?"

"No one's ever seen me the way you do."

Shay seemed as though he wanted to say more, but he simply smiled and squeezed Ollie's hand. "I see you because I want to. It's up to you how much you show me. I'm sorry I went to Corina behind your back. I won't do it again, I swear."

"I don't care if you do. Maybe it's easier that way."

"It's not. I don't want to see you through someone else's eyes."

Ollie still didn't get why Shay wanted to see him at all, but he kept that to himself and checked his watch. *Shit.* He was supposed to have brought Shay back to the venue an hour ago. "You're gonna be late."

Shay grunted. "What else is new?"

But despite his nonchalance, their time really had run out—for today, at least. Ollie reluctantly got to his feet, still clutching Shay's hand. Letting go seemed like the end of the world. What if he never got it back?

"Ollie?"

"Yeah?"

Shay chewed on his bottom lip.

Ollie rescued it from Shay's teeth without thinking, freeing it with his thumb. He lingered there, tracking Shay's tongue as it darted out to moisten his lips. "What is it?"

His whisper seemed to carry through the trees, unnaturally loud in the quiet park. Shay sucked in a breath and leaned into Ollie's touch. "I want you to kiss me again."

Another whisper. "Why?"

"Because I was drunk as fuck last time, and I need to know it was real."

"It was real."

"Ollie—"

Ollie cut Shay off, pressing their lips together in the kind of kiss that blew memories out of the sky. His head swam, and he gripped Shay's jacket and then his face, hanging on for dear life as desire swept through him. It was the best kind of heat—the *only* heat Ollie could contemplate, even as it sluiced through his senses, clearing his synapses of anything that wasn't Shay's lips on his, Shay's hands on his hips… anything that wasn't *Shay*.

It went on and on. Shay made a quiet sound—a moan, a soft gasp of pleasure—and the frigid wind that picked up around them did little to slow the stampede of sensation. Ollie's trembling became welcome, almost addictive, and it was only the incessant buzz of his phone in his pocket that forced him to stop.

Ollie pulled back and pressed their foreheads together. "It was real."

CHAPTER TEN

THE LAST Glasgow gigs passed in a flash. Shay closed the last show on Larry's favourite cajon drum and gazed out at the crowd. Faces, so many faces. He couldn't see Ollie, and Ollie hadn't even said he was coming, but he was there. Shay felt it.

And better than that, he was waiting backstage when Shay got there, his characteristic sardonic grin firmly in place.

Shay staggered towards him, his legs shaky from jumping around like a maniac for the last two hours.

Ollie caught him and gripped his chin in his hand. "You need to eat something."

He was right. Shay hadn't noticed his sugars dropping, but as the adrenaline faded, so did his equilibrium.

Ollie said something to someone nearby—Corina, maybe? Shay didn't much care—and then hauled him away to the dressing room. He deposited Shay on the couch and vanished briefly, only to reappear with Shay's medical bag.

He crouched down, his hands on Shay's knees. "What do you need?"

A giggle bubbled in Shay's chest. He tried to swallow it down, but it escaped anyway. "Sorry. Hypos make me silly sometimes."

"Uh-huh. The question still stands. What do you need?"

Despite lacking the desire to puke, faint, or fall into a coma in front of Ollie, focusing was hard. Shay's diminished senses were compounded by Ollie touching him, and he was struggling to form a coherent thought.

Ollie unzipped the bag. He retrieved the glucose monitor and held it up. "Do we do this first? Or do you need medication or food straight away?"

"We?"

"Figure of speech, dickhead."

Shay liked it when Ollie forgot himself and bantered with him like they were friends. It made the ethereal glow of the two crazy-hot kisses they'd shared seem almost normal. Manageable. Yeah, that was a better word—there was nothing normal about the way Ollie kissed him.

"*Shay.*"

Fuck. Shay made an effort to pull himself together. "I need to check my levels before I know what I need. I think it's low. It feels like a low."

"Okay. Hold out your hand."

"You're going to do it?"

"Corina showed me how last night. In case this ever happened when we were alone. She worries about you."

"That's sweet."

"It's precious. Hold out your hand."

Shay held out his hand, oddly fascinated by Ollie's earnest frown, even though he'd seen it a hundred times before, and grateful that Corina had possessed the foresight to prep Ollie on his tendency to flake after a show. Perhaps he could've stuck his own finger, but he didn't want to. He wanted Ollie to do it.

Ollie pricked Shay's finger with far more care than anyone else, Shay included, ever had. He squeezed the tiny drop of blood into the monitor, then wiped Shay's finger clean. "You'll have to tell me what the numbers mean. I haven't googled it yet."

Shay cringed. "Don't google it. I don't want you to know what a wreck I can be."

"You're joking, right?"

Shay wasn't, but he took Ollie's point. They'd hardly seen each other since their stroll in the park had turned magical, but the shift between them since that day was palpable. They weren't friends, and they weren't lovers, but they were something.

The glucose monitor beeped. Shay squinted at the numbers and forced himself to make sense of them. "I need a Lucozade. And then maybe a sandwich? One of those horrible brown ones that taste like doormats?"

"Okay, mate." Ollie chuckled and got to his feet.

He disappeared again. Shay counted his footsteps and tried to stay awake. It wasn't a dramatic low—just a blip—but it would be oh-so easy to lie down and go to sleep, let the hypo take him wherever it wanted. Not because he wanted to die or anything, but simply because he was tired.

"Shay, come on." Ollie helped Shay sit up and held a bottle of Lucozade to his lips. "Drink up. It'll make you feel better."

"I know that," Shay grumbled, but he let Ollie pour the sickly sweet drink into his mouth until he was stable enough to hold it himself.

He drained the bottle. It would take fifteen minutes or so to fully kick in, but he felt better already. He reached for Ollie. Found his hands. "Thank you."

"No worries. I'm working on that sandwich, okay? Just sit tight."

Shay curled up on the couch and watched Ollie tap out messages on his phone until Jumbo appeared with a hessian sandwich. "Last one in the petrol station. Think they reckoned I was a stoner."

"You are." Shay sat up. "Thanks, though."

"Not the point, and you're welcome." Jumbo crossed the room with the sandwich and pressed it into Shay's hand.

Standard MO would've been for him to launch it across the room, so Shay was willing to bet he still looked like warmed-up shit.

"You need anything else?" Jumbo asked.

Shay started to answer, then realised Jumbo was talking to Ollie.

Nice. And he wasn't even being sarcastic. Smuggler's Beat were a tight-knit group, and they took care of each other. That they were willing to leave Shay's babysitting to Ollie said a lot. *They like him.*

It shouldn't have mattered, but it did.

Jumbo left, probably to hit the town. Shay inhaled the sandwich and checked his levels again. *Bonza.* He was back in business. And Ollie was still with him, still crouched at Shay's feet, staring up at him like he was the only man in the world.

It was insane how radically their dynamic had shifted since Ollie had gifted Shay that tiny glimpse of himself. Nothing had really changed, but at the same time, it had changed everything. Shay looked at Ollie and saw a different man. And *Ollie* was different. Calmer, perhaps. Less intense, unless they were talking about the TV project. Then he turned crazy serious, and Shay's blood ran even hotter for him. "Um… what do you want to do now?"

"Now?"

"Yeah." Shay stretched his legs out in front of him. "The bus isn't leaving until the morning, so we could go for a drink if you want?"

Ollie pulled a face that took ten years off him. "It would turn into ten drinks, trust me, and I'm trying not to self-medicate."

"It's not easier if you're unconscious when the bus is moving?"

"You'd think it would be, but no. I've never managed to stay asleep for an entire journey, and it gets into my dreams. There's nothing like waking up sweating on a packed tour bus. You can trust me on that too."

Shay had only seen Ollie asleep once. They'd come back from rehearsal to find him knocked out on his bed, surrounded by books and work. The others hadn't paid much attention, but it had hurt Shay's heart. He'd drawn the curtain around Ollie to give him some privacy, and spent the next few hours staring at the tiny gap he'd missed. "So… no partying and eating shitty food. We can just go to bed if you want—uh—I mean, head back to the bus?"

Ollie smirked. "I know what you meant. And I'm pretty knackered, if you don't mind calling it a night?"

Shay couldn't deny the disappointment that sank through him. He hadn't seen much of Ollie since their time at the library, and with no one else around now, he'd been counting on some time alone with him. But still. Corina had booked herself into a hotel, and Smugs—the driver—had the night off. Chances were the bus would be deserted. "Let's go."

They meandered back to the bus, taking time out for Ollie to smoke. The bus was parked around the back of the gig venue, next to the Forth and Clyde Canal. In daylight, it was pretty, sunlight dappling the water through the trees. At night it was murky and bleak, and Shay felt safer with Ollie by his side.

As predicted, the bus was empty. Shay went to his bunk and checked his sugar levels again, then took a shot of insulin to last him through the night. In his peripheral vision, he tracked Ollie as he went to his own bunk, grabbed a towel and a change of clothes, and disappeared into the bathroom.

That was something else he'd noticed about Ollie as the tour had progressed. While the others—even Mara—had given up on any idea of privacy, often roaming the aisle in their pyjamas, Ollie was rarely seen without his shoes on, let alone lacking anything else. *Does he sleep in his clothes?* Shay had no idea.

He changed into the soft sweatpants he slept in, and his favourite Charlatans T-shirt. He'd cut the sleeves off a few years ago, leaving it little more than a scraggly vest, but he'd kept it to wind up his mum and couldn't bear to chuck it now.

Ollie emerged from the bathroom wearing a hoodie and jogging bottoms, his damp hair sticking up in every direction. He looked rumpled and gorgeous, and Shay couldn't bear the thought of him disappearing into his bunk.

As though he'd read Shay's mind, Ollie dumped his dirty clothes, dug his laptop from his bag, and came to Shay's bedside. "I've got some films downloaded if you're not tired enough to sleep yet. What are you into?"

Shay's heart leapt. He tossed his medical bag under his bunk and scooted over, making room for Ollie to sit down.

Ollie perched on the edge of the bed, which wasn't quite what Shay had in mind, but it would do… for now.

With the laptop positioned between them, they scrolled through the films on Ollie's hard drive. "Thought you said you had a few?" Shay opened a folder with another fifty or so movies stashed in it, all categorised by genre—apparently, Ollie was tidier with his virtual belongings than his physical ones. "There's hundreds on here."

Ollie offered a sheepish shrug. "It's my thing. At least I don't have to cart them around like the dozen or so instruments you have. And those are just what you've brought on tour with you. How many guitars do you have at home?"

"Actually, I only have a couple of guitars in my house."

Ollie cocked his head sideways. "Sounds like a technicality to me."

"If you say so." Shay kept his eyes on the screen. "Do mandolins count?"

"Yes. So do banjos, ukuleles, and any other interpretation I haven't thought of."

Shay laughed. "Busted. If we're counting all that then I have at least twenty, and, um, six woodwind instruments, fifteen drums, and an electric piano."

"Your neighbours must love you."

"Put it this way, they're glad I'm away a lot. What are your neighbours like?"

"No idea." Ollie peered over Shay's shoulder, the spicy scent of his shampoo invading Shay's senses. "I live in a tower block of new-build flats. No one knows anyone."

"That's sad."

"Not when you grow up in neighbourhoods where everyone knew if you pissed sideways. I like the anonymity."

"Why?"

Ollie shrugged. "I like my own space?"

The questioning lilt gave him away. Shay trailed a finger over the back of Ollie's hand, then turned back to the laptop screen. "Do you like Tom Hardy? Can we look in his folder?"

After a beat, Ollie snorted. "Doesn't the fact that he has his own folder give me away?"

As much as anything ever does. Shay opened the file and pointed at the film topping the list. "I haven't seen *Legend.*"

"Easily fixed."

Ollie cued up the film and slid the laptop closer to Shay. He started to stand up, but Shay caught his hand. "Watch it with me."

"Here?" Ollie glanced pointedly at Shay's bed.

"Yeah. I mean, we can go to the lounge if you want, but it's full of beer cans and crisp packets. I'd have to clean it before we sat down."

"Don't like mess, eh?"

"Not if I have to sit in it. It makes my brain too crowded."

Ollie's expression flickered. He withdrew his hand but didn't move away.

Shay shuffled even closer to the window, leaving more than enough room for Ollie to sit beside him. After a brief standoff, Ollie seemed to give in. He sighed and sat down, and the restricted space on the bunk meant he had to sit *right next* to Shay, their thighs and shoulders pressed together. It was awkward and perfect, and Shay hardly dared breathe.

The opening credits of the film filled the laptop screen. The MacBook was the newest model, and the picture was so crisp and clear Shay was instantly sucked in, but the magic of Ollie beside him didn't fade. The minutes ticked by, and the tension faded. Shay stuck his legs under the covers and wriggled down the bed. Ollie stayed on top of the thin duvet but slid to Shay's level. They stared at each other, unblinking. Then Ollie kissed Shay, just once, lightly on the lips. A featherlight split second of wonder that was over so fast Shay wondered if he'd imagined it.

Ollie drew back and lolled his head on Shay's shoulder. His breathing slowed, and his limbs relaxed. His characteristic edges softened.

He fell asleep.

CHAPTER ELEVEN

OLLIE WOKE at dawn. He was curled on his side, his face wedged between Shay's shoulder blades, one arm slung around Shay's waist, and the distinct absence of the pounding heart he usually woke up with.

He felt like he'd blinked and a lifetime had passed. As though he'd drunk twelve pints and come to on another planet. *This can't be real.* What the fuck had he been thinking? Or perhaps that was the problem. Being around Shay seemed to stop him thinking at all.

Idiot.

It took everything Ollie had to tear himself away. The bus had a heating system, but Jumbo slept next to the controls and turned it off every night. Mornings were bitter—particularly Scottish mornings—and snuggling up with Shay was apparently the cure.

Ollie rolled onto his back and then off Shay's bed. His socked feet hit the cool floor, and he found himself caught in Corina's glare. She was sitting in the office, working while she watched over the sleeping bus, like Ollie had done most nights since he'd joined the tour.

In the dim light of the early morning, she looked less than impressed to see Ollie stumbling out of Shay's bunk. "We, uh, fell asleep watching a film."

"Of course you did."

"It's true."

"It's not my business if it's not."

"Isn't it?"

Corina narrowed her eyes, frowning hard enough to draw Ollie away from Shay's bed. He padded to the kitchen and loaded the coffee machine. The temptation to take a mug back to Shay's bed was so fucking strong, but dawn had brought with it perspective, and whatever Corina was trying to convey with her glare was probably right. He had no business falling asleep in Shay's bed.

You had no business kissing him again either.

Semantics.

Ollie retreated to his own bunk, then realised he'd left his laptop behind. Under the weight of Corina's scowl, he crept back down the aisle and retrieved it from where it had become wedged between Shay's bed and the wall. Shay stirred. Ollie wanted to brush his hair out of his face and kiss his temple. He settled for drawing the curtain around him and tiptoeing away.

He sat on his bed and opened the laptop. The film from last night was still on the screen. Ollie didn't remember falling asleep, but he couldn't recall watching much of the film either, and he certainly didn't remember pausing it. If the screen was right, Shay had stopped it thirty-seven minutes in. Which meant he'd consciously let Ollie spend the rest of the night on his bed.

Ollie shivered and imagined Shay in his king-size bed in London. How they could utilise the space before they passed out wrapped up in each other. It was there; Ollie could almost taste it, but the fantasy wasn't real. In a few weeks' time, Ollie would go home alone, and Shay would carry on living his best life.

And it was better that way... for everyone.

For long minutes, Ollie was almost convinced as he stared at a freeze-framed Tom Hardy, but his heart protested, and the conflict raging inside made his skin burn all over again. *Fuck, fuck, fuck.* It was moments like these when Ollie wanted to die. Fleeting flashes of absolute despair. They always faded to a dull roar of misery, but they hurt all the same.

He rubbed his chest and opened up the research document he needed for his next session with Shay. Corina couldn't spare him until they reached Sunderland, but they had shows booked in Newcastle first. A week ago, Ollie would've left the tour and gone home, rejoining at the last possible opportunity. Now he wanted to run home so badly his bones ached, but the pull of the sleeping man two beds away was stronger.

Wasn't it?

"We can do it ourselves," Shay said. "I don't get what the problem is."

Jumbo flicked a balled-up crisp packet at him. "That's because you've never had to haul your own kit around. If we have to lug our gear onto every stage for the next few weeks, I guarantee someone—probably you—is gonna drop down dead."

Ollie winced. Jumbo was hardly known for his tact, but that was a low blow. Shay managed his condition as well as he could on the road, and he had more energy on stage than any performer Ollie had ever seen. Certainly more than Jumbo, who had a tendency to hide behind his double bass.

He did have a point, though. Losing their roadie squad to a postpub squabble meant extra hours before and after each show, more stress, and less time to recuperate between gigs. They were stretched thin as it was.

The band continued to bicker. Ollie kept his head down. The bus was on the road, and he'd sensed Shay watching him since he'd woken up an hour ago, but for the first time in a while, he had the monster under control. Had it trapped in the corner while he fed it scraps of anxiety and got on with his work. He couldn't deny that the argument going on around him helped.

Or that witnessing Shay lose his temper was shamefully hot.

Knew he was a firecracker.

Ollie opened his emails. He ignored most of them and clicked on the latest one from his boss, asking him how he was getting on, and questioning why his expense receipts totalled next to nothing when the last dude they'd sent on a band tour had spent half a year's salary on booze.

Morning, Amir,

Project is going fine, thanks. Shay is responding well on film, and the research is holding up. Doing some more digging on the road, and hope to finish up in Leeds at the end of the tour.

Ollie

The tour actually concluded in Derby—Shay's home city—but Ollie had been unable to find a connection to the city that wasn't tied to his adoptive parents. He sent the email, not expecting a reply anytime soon from Amir's saturated inbox.

An email pinged straight back.

Ollie, I know all that. I was more interested in your welfare.

Amir

Ollie sighed. Amir was a great boss on a creative level—his predilection for giving Ollie free rein on fluid projects was the reason Ollie had signed with Sky—but emotionally he was a pain in the arse.

My welfare is just fine, thanks.

Ollie

"Hey."

Ollie glanced up. Shay was standing beside the office table he was working at. "Hey, yourself. Did you win?"

"Win what?"

"The row about playing roadie for the rest of the tour."

"There was nothing to win. We either do it ourselves and fuck it up, or we get strangers in who might fuck it up too."

Ollie closed his laptop. "I thought the crew who quit were Jumbo's cousins?"

"They were."

"So hiring people you know didn't work out either?"

"I didn't know them." Shay flopped into the seat opposite.

"But Jumbo wanted to do them a favour, and I agreed because I'm a pushover. Finn told me not to do shit like that."

"Finn?"

"McGovern," Shay clarified. "We opened for The Lamps last summer."

Ollie swallowed hard. Finn McGovern had been the first rock star he'd ever crushed on. "If that had happened a few years earlier, I might've seen you play. I went to every Lamps gig I could, back in the day. What are they up to now?"

"Writing, I think. You could ask Ben, though. He played with them for a while a few years back, but Finn goes off radar sometimes, so he might not know either."

Ollie could relate to that. He'd spent a whole year playing hermit. "So… what *are* you going to do about the roadie situation? Jumbo was being a dick about it, but he kind of had a point."

"What point was that? That I'm too sickly to move my own equipment around?"

"No, that was the dick part. I meant that it's too much for all of you while you're working full-time on gigging."

"Lots of bands do it and get by. We're not precious, Ollie."

"Doesn't mean you can't look for a better way. Do you have a budget to hire a new crew?"

Shay winced. "That's the other thing. We ran way over on studio time when we recorded the album, so our support budget for the tour was cut. We hired Jumbo's cousin because he was cheap, and we paid them up front, in cash, with no contract. Even if we get someone else in, I don't know who the fuck's gonna pay them."

"Isn't this Corina's problem?"

"You'd think, but she never sanctioned the cash payment, and she said it's not her job to fix our juvenile bullshit."

Ollie drummed his fingers on the table. The three-hour journey from Glasgow to Newcastle was relatively short compared to the mammoth run down to Bristol they had coming up, but without his work, and the band bickering at top volume to distract him, anxiety was beginning to claw at his guts. "Have you got enough cash between you to pay anyone else at all?"

Shay slumped forwards, head on his arms. "Maybe a couple, but we had four guys before. I don't think two could handle it."

"I can help."

"Help?"

"Yeah, I can move shit around before and after your gigs. It'll give me something to do."

"Don't try and convince me you haven't got enough of your own work to keep yourself occupied."

"But when does it stop?" Ollie leaned forwards, dropping his face so it was inches from Shay, so close he could've stuck his tongue out and licked Shay's full lips. "Sometimes I work because it keeps my brain quiet."

"That's not healthy."

"Never said it was, but maybe lugging your bazillion instruments around will give me some perspective, eh?"

Shay didn't seem convinced, but the bus was exiting the motorway to stop at a service station, and the rest of the band was on them before he could respond.

Jumbo stomped past without looking at them. Mara grabbed Shay's arm and hustled him off the bus, which left Ollie to catch a smoke with Ben.

They took a walk to the burger van at the back of the car park. Ben lit up and blew out an exasperated lungful of smoke. "Sorry about the drama, mate."

"Don't apologise. I'm sure most bands have issues on the road."

"Yeah, we try not to be like most bands, though. And Shay didn't deserve to cop it from Jumbo. None of this is his fault."

A bristle of defensiveness ran through Ollie. He didn't need Ben to tell him that Jumbo had been a prick to Shay. Or a reminder of how it had made *him* feel. Jumbo was a big guy—*obviously*—but Ollie could happily deck him if he upset Shay again. "I told Shay I could pitch in with lifting the gear if you can club together and get a couple of guys in. Actually, come to think of it, where *is* your gear?"

Ben winced. "Still in Glasgow. Jumbo's cousin left the van in the car park and got the train home."

"And no one thought to retrieve it?"

"Dude, we only found out half an hour ago."

"So someone has to go back and get it in time for tonight's show?"

Ben lit another cigarette. "Actually, we can get away with it tonight—it's an acoustic set at an open studio, so we can use all their kit—but we're playing a winter festival tomorrow afternoon, and we're the only band on the bill, so if we don't get it back by then, we're fucked."

Ollie could see where this was going. The band's missing equipment wasn't his problem any more than it was apparently Corina's, but with her MIA, he was the only one with the time to hoof it to Glasgow and back again.

"No fucking way," Shay growled when they got back on the bus. "It's not your job to clean up our mess, and we can't afford to pay you anyway. If you'd stuck around earlier, I'd have told you that."

"I don't need you to pay me. Sky is paying me enough for this gig, considering the amount of time I spend doing fuck all."

"I've never seen you doing fuck all, and you told me from the start that you couldn't afford to lose this job."

"I wasn't talking in monetary terms." Ollie snuck a quick glance at Ben, who had suddenly found the coffee machine fascinating. "Unless you mean yours, because if you're not ready for the festival tomorrow, you'll blow your contract with that promoter. That shit ruins bands."

"It's true," Ben said. "I know we say we aren't in it for the cash, but we need to make a living, and we can't do that if we trash this tour. We're not Metallica. The record company will drop us for sure."

Shay shot him a sour look. "Metallica? Seriously? That's what you're going with?"

"I was comparing clout not musical styles."

The conversation was going nowhere. Jumbo had remained stubbornly silent, Larry was Switzerland, and Mara had sided with Corina and disappeared in a taxi.

Ollie stood and picked up his bag. "Look, you need that gear, and I've got time to fetch it. Jumbo, give me the spare keys for the van."

"No."

"Yes."

"*No*," Shay echoed. "If anyone should go, it's Jumbo. He's the fuck-up."

"And you're the one too busy bitching at your boyfriend to let him get on with it."

It was a mutinous mumble Jumbo had likely regretted the moment it was out of his mouth, but it was too late. Shay lunged at him, only to be caught by Ben.

No one caught Ollie.

Ollie grabbed Jumbo's collar and slammed him against the wall hard enough to shake the bus. "Give me the keys."

Winded, Jumbo nodded and retrieved the keys from his pocket. He handed them over, eyes downcast. "Sorry. I didn't mean that."

"Couldn't give a fuck, mate. See you later."

Ollie took the keys and jogged off the bus. Footsteps followed him. He expected Shay, but it was Larry.

"Don't mind Jumbo," he said. "He's upset about falling out with his kin. He didn't mean nothing by all that. He's gotta lot of time for you, and he loves Shay."

Ollie shouldered his bag and looked around for a bench he could park on while he figured out the least painful way to get back to Glasgow. "I don't care what Jumbo thinks of me. And even if I did, me and Shay are just... friends."

A tic in Larry's jaw caught the infinitesimal hesitation. "That ain't even the point. We all know Shay swings both ways, and it's cool. It's always been cool."

"So what is the point?" Ollie's patience expired. "You got something else you want to say, Larry?"

"It's none of my business."

It really wasn't, but the masochist in Ollie couldn't let either of them off the hook. He waited, eyebrows raised, until Larry admitted defeat and sighed.

He took his hat off and rubbed a hand over his head. "Look, I don't care what you young guns get up to when it's all gravy, I just don't want to see that boy get hurt again. His last fella was a git to him, left him hanging, and it weren't fair."

"What's that got to do with me?"

"Nothing, if the restlessness I see in you is all in my pickled old head."

"How pickled are you?" Ollie was being insolent now, but he couldn't stop, because even if Larry didn't know whether his warnings bore any weight, Ollie knew they did. Fetching the equipment would do Shay a favour, but there was no denying Ollie craved the solitude of the mission too. That even the prospect of a taxi ride back to Glasgow wasn't enough to temper the urge to flee.

I need to stop kissing him.

CHAPTER TWELVE

By the time Shay had disentangled himself from band politics, Ollie had disappeared. Shay checked the service station, McDonalds, and a nearby bus stop, but he was nowhere to be found.

"Why are you so angsty about this?" Ben said. "I know it takes the piss, but we'll make it up to him when he gets back. And whatever she's saying right now, you know Corina will pay him."

Money was the last thing on Shay's mind, but he wasn't about to tell Ben that travelling back to Glasgow by road was Ollie's worst nightmare, especially as he still didn't know why.

They trudged back to the bus. Shay's feet seemed heavier with every step, as though his body was rejecting the prospect of leaving Ollie behind. *He probably already left.* But it still hurt. More than it should've and perhaps even more than the dismay on Ollie's face when Jumbo had called Shay his boyfriend. *Yeah. That was a cracker.*

The bus hit the road. Shay retreated to his bed and tried not to let his imagination convince him he could smell Ollie on his pillow. He curled up with his notebooks and wrote some angry lyrics that were so far off-brand for Smuggler's Beat they made him laugh. *Maybe I need an emo metal band on the side.*

"Shay?"

His mind still running angsty rhymes, Shay glanced up. Jumbo was beside his bed, dressed in a onesie that made him look like a teddy bear who'd lost its mother. "What do you want, J? I'm tired, man."

"I know. I'm sorry."

"What for?"

Jumbo shrugged. "For being a cockhead?"

"You're always a cockhead. This shit was different."

"I know that too." Jumbo motioned for Shay to budge up and folded his large frame onto Shay's bed, crushing him with a warmth that had nothing on Ollie's sinewy arms wrapped around him. "And I'm sorry me and Tuffers got lairy with each other. It's the sniff, mate. You know it sends me crackers."

Shay sighed. He wasn't stupid—he knew Jumbo had been partying way too hard since they'd left home. But the band had a no-drugs clause in their contract. If Corina found out Jumbo and his boys had been rinsing coke, they'd all be stuffed. "I need you to calm the fuck down. If you keep messing up, you're going to do us all out of a job."

"Not you. The record company would never let you go."

"Even if that's true—which it's not—what about the others? You think Larry wants to go back to being a session musician? He loves the band. And what about Corina? And even Smugs? You think he gets paid if the tour gets cancelled?"

Jumbo mumbled something. Shay wasn't done, but the will to chew Jumbo out faded as sharply as it had arrived. Another sigh escaped him, and he cast his gaze around the bus, searching for Ollie's dark head even though he *knew* he wasn't there. Was the rest of the tour going to be like this? Ollie coming and going, and Shay getting whiplash trying to cope with it? The emo band was becoming more appealing by the day. *God, I'm pathetic.*

Tired of his own head, Shay leaned on Jumbo, letting the big man put his arm around him. "I kind of want to kill you," he admitted.

"I know." Jumbo squeezed him. "But I reckon you'll have to get in line. Ollie's fierce, eh?"

"Is that your way of apologising for being a twat to him too?"

"It's me practicing for when I see him, but yeah, I'm sorry about that too. I didn't mean what I said, and even if I had, I wouldn't think you and Ollie together was a bad thing. I like him."

"You don't like anyone I—"

"I didn't like the last mope you were with because he was a douche canoe. If you rocked up with someone half-decent, I'd bake you a fucking cake."

In spite of himself, Shay laughed. "You're such a poet."

"Aye, that's why we leave the lyrics to you, but I'm serious, man. I like Ollie, and he scared the fuck out of me when he booted me across the bus."

He'd scared the shit out of Shay, too, even though Shay's intention had been to attempt the same. "I think he could take you."

Jumbo grunted his agreement. "Anyway. I'm sorry I'm a prick, and you forgive me, which means we can talk about the rest of it now."

"The rest of it?"

"Uh-huh. Now I'm back in your good books, I want to know what's really going on between you and the ninja cameraman."

"You're not back in my good books. Even if you're sorry enough to climb into bed with me, you're still going to cost us a fortune in roadie fees."

"Don't worry about that. I'll cover it."

"How? You spend every penny we earn on partying."

"*Shay*. I'll sort it, okay? I'm going to be on my best behaviour from now on. Don't change the subject."

Shay took refuge under Jumbo's side and groaned. "Stop talking. Can't you just pay your penance and be my human pillow?"

Jumbo laughed. "Nope. I promised your ma I'd always interfere in your love life on her behalf, so here I am."

Shay could believe that. His mother had adored Jumbo—mostly because he'd eaten her out of house and home every time he'd come round, and he'd called her Mrs Maloney for the entire decade he'd been in Shay's life. "Don't use my dead mother to bully me."

"You really don't want to talk about it?"

Shay raised his head. It was on the tip of his tongue to rebuke Jumbo again, but there was something else too. Something that felt not unlike the constant war he fought with his pancreas. Being diabetic was like chasing a never-ending beam of light. It was always there, but he rarely caught up with it. Understanding Ollie had become just as frustrating. Consuming. And a battle he'd likely never win. "I've only known him a few weeks."

Jumbo didn't blink. "So? Didn't your parents get married a month after they met? Maybe it's in the blood to know how you feel about someone the moment you meet them."

"I'm not my parents, and blood-wise, I never will be. Besides, I have zero idea how I feel about Ollie. Just that I feel... I don't know. Fucking upside down every time I look at him."

"Okay, first of all, I wasn't talking about literal blood. More that your parents raised you to be honest with your emotions. Secondly, it's no surprise Ollie turns you upside down. The dude is a closed book. I can't even get him to tell me what beer he likes."

Shay's head was too fuzzy to make sense of Jumbo's cereal-box psychology. "How is that related?"

"Think about it, mate. If he can't let even the small shit go, how hard do you think it is for him to talk about stuff that matters?"

Jumbo grinned like he'd brought world peace to the table, but Shay wanted to cry. Because Ollie *had* told him stuff that mattered, and Shay still didn't know him at all.

"I don't think he likes me like that anyway," Shay said after a while. "Did you see his face when you called me his boyfriend?"

Jumbo winced. "I did, but it didn't make me think he didn't want what I said to be true."

"No? So what did it make you think?"

"That I'd pulled an alpha wolf's tail and I was about to get killed. Shay, I don't know where you've been your whole life—actually, I do, but that's not the point."

"Then what is the point?"

Jumbo fixed Shay with a level stare. "Basically, mate, there's no way Ollie wanted to punch my lights out for his benefit. He wanted to hurt me because I hurt you, and if that doesn't mean something, I'll eat my fucking shoe."

NEWCASTLE WAS shit. The venue was shit, the food was shit, and to top it off, Corina had ripped them all a new one so deep Shay didn't know how they'd made it out of the dressing room alive.

He retreated to a quiet corner with the worst chicken salad in the world and his phone. The temptation to stew long and hard over whether to call Ollie or not was strong, so he bit the bullet and called before it took hold.

Ollie didn't answer.

Depressed, Shay ate as much of the bad salad as he could stomach and then drifted off to find an instrument to pour his extra feelings into. It was a thing. It had always been *his* thing. He found a mandolin and an empty room and locked himself away, but the melancholy tunes he was searching for wouldn't come.

Bright chords filled the room, attacking Shay from every corner. Every stroke of his fingers across the strings made him cringe, but he couldn't seem to stop. He stomped his foot on a wooden desk, and played and played and played, and just when he feared his brain would explode, his phone rang.

Startled, Shay whirled around, searching for where he'd discarded it in favour of the mandolin. It was on the windowsill. He made a grab for it just as it rang out.

Ollie.

Fuck.

Shay called him right back, praying he'd answer.

He did. "Yeah?"

Thank God. Relief swept over Shay, and he swayed on his feet. "You answered."

"Um… why wouldn't I?"

"Because I'm a drama queen?"

"Are you?"

"Yes. No. Fuck off."

"You called me."

"You called me first."

"Nope. You rang me while I was losing my mind in a taxi. I reckoned I'd wait until I'd had a few smokes before I called back. Sorry I kept you hanging."

Shay sat down abruptly on a hard plastic chair. "Shit, I'm sorry. Was the journey really bad?"

"Yeah. Cars are the worst for me. Believe it or not, I actually do okay on the bus compared to this."

"I wish you'd tell me why."

"So do I, mate."

"Really?"

Ollie sighed. "Of course I do. I'm not hiding my whole self from you on purpose. It's just when I try and bring stuff together to talk about it, nothing comes out."

It was coming out now, whether Ollie realised it or not. Perhaps he was too rattled to filter himself. Or maybe he'd simply given up trying. Whatever. Shay sucked up every stray revelation and stashed it away. "I'm so sorry you had to do this. Jumbo apologised to me on the way here. He's a twat, but he doesn't mean to be. I think he's been partying too hard."

Ollie laughed softly. "I figured as much. Maybe I shouldn't have gone at him, but there's something about you, Shay. I wanted to kill him. Just for a second, but I really did."

"I get it," Shay said. "I wanted to deck him myself for being such a prick to you. This isn't what you signed up for."

"It isn't, but I'm not complaining. The taxi ride was shitty, but fetching the van gives me something to do. It's when I'm bored that my life gets really fucked up."

Shay's heart hurt. Ollie was such a contradiction—steely and strong, but fragile in ways most people would never know. They were barely scratching the surface, and perhaps this was as far as he'd ever let Shay in, but God, Shay felt every ounce of pain in Ollie's rough voice. "When will you be back?"

"Depends on traffic, but probably around eight?"

"We'll be on stage by then."

"I know. Maybe I'll catch the show."

"I hope so."

"Me too. Are you okay?"

"Hmm?" Startled, Shay stood and walked to the wall where a window might've been had he not been buried in the depths of the venue. "Me? Why are you asking that?"

"Because you sound fed up… and because I want to know."

It was Shay's turn to sigh. "That's sweet, but yeah, I'm fine. I'm just pissed off that everything's turned to shit. And I'm hungry. The food here is wank."

Ollie laughed again, properly this time, and it was as if he'd injected it right into Shay's veins. Warmth and light spread through Shay, even though he was still alone in the chilly, dark room. "I know Newcastle pretty well, as it goes. I've got family up there, and my cousin happens to have a shop just up the road from where you are."

"I'm listening."

"It's one of those Polish shops that sells everything but the kitchen sink, and right at the back, he has a hot plate that'll sort you right out… I mean, if you're up for a walk?"

After hours of windowless solitude, Shay couldn't think of anything better. He picked up the mandolin and strummed a few mindless cords.

"'Country Girl'?" Ollie said.

"Huh?"

"You're playing it."

"Am I?" Shay repeated the chords and played some more. Then it clicked, and it dawned on him that he'd spent his entire afternoon murdering Primal Scream. *Jesus, where's my head at?* "I didn't even realise."

"You're funny."

"Not on purpose."

Ollie laughed some more, then gave Shay directions to his cousin's shop and precise instructions on what to buy. "Trust me," he said. "If you're hungry and cranky, the goulash and cabbage will sort you right out."

Shay believed him. "Thanks. I'm going to go now. Um… are you going to be around after the show?"

There was a pause, and then the flick of a cigarette lighter. Ollie blew out smoke, and it seemed like a lifetime passed before he spoke again. "I'll find you, Shay. I promise."

CHAPTER THIRTEEN

The problem with promises was that even the ones you meant most were impossible to keep when the world worked against you. Ollie glared at the car park barrier holding the van hostage with increasing dismay. According to the signage, it lifted at midnight.

"Seriously?" he muttered. "What kind of fucking goth car park opens at midnight?"

The one Jumbo's cousin had dumped the van in, apparently. Ollie wondered if Shay had ever known quite how far from the venue the band's highly valuable stage gear had been kept. Considered telling him, then changed his mind. Shay had sounded stressed enough on the phone, which made the pull to get back to him ache even harder.

Ollie scrubbed a hand over his face. Midnight. Damn. That meant he wouldn't hit Newcastle till three in the morning. Would Shay even be awake? If he was, chances were he'd be drunk, though Ollie was willing to bet Corina had put the kibosh on that shit for a while.

With heavy legs, Ollie slipped under the barrier and approached the van. It was a rusty white transit, but a glance under the bonnet and a kick of the tyres convinced him it wasn't a death trap. Shame it wasn't going anywhere soon.

It had been a few months since Ollie had last driven. Living in the city meant he spent his life on the Tube or on foot, but he liked driving when his mood was right. It was probably the only time he ever felt as though he'd won.

He checked his watch. Seven hours till he could hit the road, and he still hadn't told Shay. Sighing, he fished his phone from his back pocket. It was habit to keep it on silent, so he hadn't heard Shay's message come through. It was a picture of a bowl of Ollie's family goulash, and his stomach growled even as his heart clenched a little.

Ollie: *Did you speak to Agnes?*

Shay: *no, it was a fella who served me. i said i knew you tho. think that's why they gave me enough for 75 million people*

Ollie was too behind on family gossip to know immediately who the man who'd served Shay could've been, but picturing Shay among them felt… nice. Right. And terrifying enough for him to push it from his mind.

Ollie: *So… I have news….*

Shay: *good or bad?*

Ollie: *Both.*

Shay: *good news first, i'm too happy in my lonely meat coma*

Ollie: *I found the van.*

Shay: *okaaaaaaay. bad news?*

Ollie: *It wasn't at the venue. It's locked in a car park down the road and I can't get it back till midnight.*

Shay didn't reply straight away. Ollie locked the van and dropped his phone in his pocket, thankful he'd had the neurotic foresight to bring his laptop. He had a shit-ton of editing to do, and it was the closest he was going to get to Shay for a while.

Lacking any better ideas, he returned to the cafe that had used to house Rudolph Kaspersen's hardware store. Luckily for him, it stayed open until late, and the all-day breakfast called his name. He snapped a picture for Shay, who still hadn't read his last message, and drank as much coffee as he dared before he opened the video-editing software that fluctuated between being the finest technology ever invented and the bane of his life.

Today turned out to be a bane of his life day. Glitches, bugs, missing actions—nothing worked the way it should, and he was on the verge of hurling the whole lot through the cafe window when his phone flashed.

Shay: *but you are coming back, right?*

Ollie frowned. Why would Shay ask him that when he had thousands of pounds worth of equipment to return to the band? Did he seriously think Ollie was going to pull a fast one and flog it on eBay?

It's not the gear he's worried about, knobhead.

But that realisation made Ollie frown even harder. He was self-aware enough to know his flip-flop moods and mixed messages were likely giving Shay a migraine, but to think Ollie would duck out on him now?

You would. You still might.

The demon was loud—too loud. Ollie shut his laptop without saving any of the tenuous progress he'd made and stood with a screech of his chair. He stuffed his laptop into his backpack and tossed way too much money on the table.

Fuck car park barriers, he was getting out of here.

<hr>

OLLIE SLIPPED a grateful fifty-pound note to the car park attendant and burned under the raised barrier. He navigated out of the city and hit the main road south, absorbed in the absolute mess of the van's cab. Litter, partying detritus, even a half-eaten Fray Bentos pie, but he didn't care. In the two hours it had taken him to track down the company managing the car park and persuade them to let him out, the pull to be with Shay had become desperate.

So much so that he'd forgotten to text him back, but there wasn't much he could do about that now. Besides. It was nine o'clock. Shay was on stage.

Ollie fiddled with the radio. As luck would have it, it somehow picked up the northern radio station that was broadcasting the Newcastle gig. Ollie's heart skipped a beat as the presenter cut the commercials and announced the band. He'd heard them play live a few times now, and seen them rehearse more than he could count, but this was different. Stripped back and acoustic, this was Smuggler's Beat as he'd never heard them before.

This was *Shay* as he'd never heard him before.

The road faded as the gig played out. Shay's voice filled Ollie's every sense and drove him on, his foot pressing harder to the accelerator with each track. The band had a dozen instruments that they swapped around whenever the fancy took them, but Ollie knew when it was Shay playing. Knew which notes came from his heart and the drumbeats that came from his soul.

His voice was different too. It had always been raw, but now every song had an edge Ollie couldn't describe, a depth that pulled him under, and by the time he rolled into Newcastle, he felt as though he'd combust if he didn't get to Shay soon.

It was two o'clock in the morning. Road closures and a wonky sat nav had sent him round in circles, and he wasn't much earlier than if he'd waited until midnight to leave. But still. He was here. He had to hope that Shay hadn't given up on him and hit the town.

Ollie parked the van and slid out of the driver's seat, his legs stiff from being behind the wheel so long. The bus was close by, no lights or signs of life. Ollie had a fob that unlocked the living quarters, but he found the door unlocked. He crept up the steps, expecting a row of empty bunks, but as his vision cleared, he realised the whole band was present, correct—and fast asleep in their beds.

Even Jumbo.

Wow. It didn't take a genius to figure that Corina had reasserted her authority. Ollie half expected to find her sitting at the office desk, watching over them like a matron, but she wasn't. In fact, she was nowhere around at all. She rarely slept on the bus, a fact Ollie was glad of as he ditched his bag and his boots and tiptoed to Shay's bunk.

Shay's curtains were open, and he was curled on his side, one arm pillowing his head, the other flung out as though he was searching for something. His hand dangled over the side. Ollie grasped it and entwined their fingers. He thought about leaning down and kissing him but settled for whispering Shay's name until he stirred.

"Ollie?"

"It's me." Ollie squeezed Shay's hand a little tighter. "The van's safe, your gear's safe."

Shay stared at him, his sleepy eyes a mix of relief and confusion. He tugged Ollie closer until Ollie was all but lying on top of him.

Then he kissed Ollie's cheek, his jaw, his lips. "I don't care about the gear."

A shiver ran through Ollie, but for once it was the good kind —the kind only Shay had ever elicited from him. Kissing Shay back was easy. Giving in to slide onto his bed, to mould their bodies together as their tongues fought for dominance, even more so.

Shay was shirtless. Ollie ran his hands all over his smooth skin, all the while praying Shay wouldn't try to do the same to him. As he found Shay's sensitive spots and committed them to memory, the worry slipped further from his mind, but it was there —fuck, it was always there.

He buried his face in Shay's neck, kissing the delicate flesh, revelling in Shay's pleasured gasp. *God, I want him.* And right now, Ollie wasn't in the mood to remember that the roadblocks he'd set up in his mind would ensure that it could never happen. Right now he wanted to pretend they were both undamaged and whole, and losing himself in Shay's gorgeous body was the best distraction.

Whether it was instinct or the fact that he'd just woken up, Shay kept his exploration of Ollie tame. As he arched beneath Ollie, his long fingers remained buried in Ollie's hair, and despite every ruined nerve crying out for Shay's touch, Ollie was so fucking glad, he wanted to cry. *Please. Just let us have this.*

Shay's sweatpants slid down his hips, lower and lower. His

hard length pressed against Ollie's thigh, and Ollie's mouth watered.

He slipped a hand under Shay's waistband. "Is this okay?"

"Shut the curtain."

Ollie obeyed and, as he came upright, found himself level with Shay's groin. The sweatpants were gone.

Desire surged through Ollie. He took Shay in his mouth, swallowing him with little warning. Shay shuddered, his groan muffled by the pillow he pulled over his face. His thighs trembled, and Ollie made the most of how wound up he was.

It was quick.

Brutal, almost.

Ollie worked Shay, drinking in everything he got in return— every muted gasp and strangled moan, every jerk and shiver. He pinned Shay to the narrow bed, hands clawing at his slim hips. Tenderness dissolved into a frenetic rhythm. Heat sluiced through Ollie, and he welcomed the sharp sting of Shay tugging at his hair.

Shay came.

Stars exploded.

Ollie smiled and felt whole.

He crawled up the bed. Shay reached for him. "Let me—"

Ollie cut him off with a kiss, guiding Shay's hands away from where he wanted them most. *Please don't.*

Shay didn't. He kissed Ollie until they ran out of air, then broke away with a jaw-popping yawn.

He laid his head on Ollie's chest. Ollie tangled his fingers in Shay's hair and stared at the ceiling. "I was in an accident a few years ago... a car accident."

Shay froze but didn't speak.

Ollie sucked in a breath and carried on. "I was a passenger in an Uber coming back into London from Oxford after a meeting. The car flipped on the M1 and burst into flames. The driver died, and my left side got burned to fuck. I don't remember much, or what happened after, but my body won't ever forget."

He nudged Shay, forcing him to meet his gaze. "I've never

shown anyone what's left of me, not even my mum. And I don't know how to fix that."

Shay swallowed hard, a tremor running through his slim frame. "It wouldn't change how I saw you."

"It's changed how you see me already. I can tell."

"Ollie—"

"Shh." Ollie tapped his finger to Shay's lips. "I don't want sympathy. I just need you to know why I am how I am. So you never think it's your fault."

"But—"

Ollie shook his head. "Go back to sleep, okay? I'll stay with you, I promise."

CHAPTER FOURTEEN

SHAY WAS stuck in a twilight zone where Ollie handed out brain-melting blow jobs with one hand and devastating bombshells with the other. Also, in the cold light of the early morning, the possibility that he'd dreamed some of it was totally a thing. Only the fact that Ollie lay asleep beside him made it seem real.

Ollie was fully clothed and on top of the duvet. Shay scowled. It was too cold for that shit, and he wanted to cuddle against Ollie's back without freezing to death. He sat up and reached for a hoodie, prepared to sacrifice the covers for the opportunity to wrap his arms around Ollie.

The bus doors opened and closed as he was slipping it over his head. Light footsteps tapped down the aisle. *Corina.* She poked her head around Shay's curtain and rolled her eyes. She disappeared, only to return with the duvet from the bunk she rarely slept in.

Shay opened his mouth to thank her.

She tapped her lips and vanished.

Problem solved, Shay spread the duvet over the narrow bunk and lay back down, grateful that Ollie's jeans were so battered they were nice and soft, and that the lack of space meant he could press up close to him without looking like a needy weirdo.

You are a needy weirdo.

Whatever.

Exhausted from travelling, performing, and angsting over Ollie, it didn't take Shay long to drift back to sleep. The warmth of Ollie in his arms was soothing, and his heart quieted. Maybe when it was really morning they could get breakfast and talk some more. Or maybe not.

Maybe Ollie was done talking and what he'd already said would be enough.

OLLIE WAS awake. Shay knew it like he knew the draught torturing his exposed bare foot was coming from the fucking Arctic. But he didn't move. Didn't dare. At some point they'd shifted on the bed, rolling over so Ollie was behind him, arms vice-like around Shay's waist, his morning wood deliciously hard against Shay's leg. *I want to stay like this forever.*

But wishful thinking got Shay nowhere. A few blissful seconds later, Ollie kissed the back of Shay's neck and rolled away.

Shay played possum while Ollie sat up and did something with the curtain. He wondered if Ollie would slip away like he had the last time they'd shared a bed. When he didn't immediately disappear, Shay took a chance, turned over, and opened his eyes.

Ollie was staring right at him, his expression as unguarded as Shay had ever seen it. *It really happened.*

Shay blinked as images of Ollie lying helpless in the back of a car, surrounded by smoke, blood, and flames flashed, unbidden, through his mind. He couldn't imagine pain like that, or what it did to a man. Ollie had said it had happened a few years ago. Perhaps his physical wounds had healed, but Ollie hadn't. Shay's heart cried out. *I'm so sorry this happened to you.* "You stayed," he said stupidly instead.

Ollie said nothing. Just tucked a stray lock of hair behind Shay's ear, but that he made no move to leave the bed was everything.

Shay found his hand and squeezed. "Lie down again?"

Ollie shrugged. "If you want." He slid down the bed as though they woke up like this every morning. And if he noticed the multiplying duvets, it didn't show.

Shay wasn't in the mood for a loaded silence, so he found the news channel on his phone and propped it up on the shelf. It was the smallest makeshift TV in the world, but it did the job, and with the scent of coffee drifting past the curtain from whoever had ventured out of bed first, he could almost pretend they were at home. His home. Ollie's home. Didn't matter.

Reality was never far away, though. Shay reached for his medical bag and dug out the glucose monitor. He wasn't in the mood for this shit either, but it was one of the few things in life he'd never be able to choose his way out of.

Ollie took the kit from him. "I can do it."

It was the first time he'd spoken. His voice was raspy, but present, and relief flowed through Shay. Last night, when he'd been talking about the... accident, he'd sounded so distant Shay had irrationally wanted to shake him. As though Ollie detaching himself from something so horrific was somehow unreasonable. "You don't have to."

"I know." Ollie moved deftly to draw blood from Shay's finger and feed it onto the test strip. "But I reckon you must get fed up with it."

"Not as much as when I was growing up. I used to drive my ma mad back then. My fourteen-year-old self would rather have risked a hypo than stop what I was doing for this rubbish."

"Sounds legit."

"I thought so. The hospital said I qualify for an insulin pump, but I haven't got around to thinking about it properly."

"Why not?"

"I'm busy. And lazy. And I'm not sure I want a permanent reminder of my wonky system attached to myself. At least the old-fashioned way I get a few hours where I can forget about it."

"I never thought of it like that. Your reading is 4.1. Is that okay?"

Shay nodded. "It'll do. I should probably eat soon, though."

"Soon?"

"Yeah. As in I'm not getting out of bed until I absolutely have to."

Ollie grinned faintly. "Sounds good to me."

"Does it?"

"Yes, Shay. It does."

"You're staring," Jumbo said.

"Am not."

"You bloody are. Everything okay?"

Shay tore his gaze from where Ollie was preparing to set off in the van for the next tour stop in Sunderland. He looked considerably more cheerful about it than he had any other leg of the journey, and now Shay knew why, he couldn't stop thinking about it. "I'm fine."

"I didn't mean just you, mate."

Shay rolled his eyes. Jumbo, still buoyed by guilt over fucking the roadie situation and being a general pain in the arse, had been glued to his side since Ollie had left the bus. "What did you mean, then?"

"Nothing specific. I saw Ollie rolling out of your bed for the second day straight this morning, and now you're being all emo and shit, so...."

Shay scowled. He'd spent the last few weeks accusing himself of the same thing, but he wasn't about to take it from Jumbo, even if the big man did seem to have his hooligan heart in the right place. "Forget what I told you the other day, okay? I don't want to talk about it."

"Do you want a hug?"

"Piss off."

Jumbo grinned and shuffled away, and Shay continued to study Ollie. It was lunchtime, and after a hectic schedule the previous day, the entire bus had spent most of the morning in bed.

Shay and Ollie had holed up behind the curtain, watching the news play on a loop while they held hands, gazed at each other, and hardly spoke. It had been perfect but, as ever, had left Shay pondering what the hell would happen next. Was Ollie going to slide so easily into Shay's bed every evening? Last night he'd swapped his jeans for sweatpants, and there'd been no repeat of *that* blow job, but nothing else had been different. They'd still held each other like lovers all night long.

Ollie glanced up. He wouldn't be able to see Shay through the blacked-out bus windows, but Shay felt his gaze on him all the same, and sat down so he couldn't see Ollie either. Somewhere on his bed, his phone rang. Shay searched half-heartedly for it and found it beneath his pillow as the call rang out.

Dammit. He'd been meaning to have a proper conversation with his dad for days, and right now, with a thirty-minute trip to Sunderland to kill, he had time to speak for longer than the usual three-and-a-half minutes.

He called his father back. "Hey."

"All right, lad?"

Frank Maloney's gruff voice was like a blanket and a book on a cold winter day. Shay lay back on his bed—he definitely could smell Ollie this time—and folded his free arm behind his head. "What are you up to?"

"Walking the hounds. I thought I'd try out that flash new phone you sent me so I could talk to you when I was out."

"It's not flash, Dad. It's the oldest iPhone in the world."

"Not as old as me, though, eh?"

"You're not that old."

"Feel it, son, without your mother here nagging me along."

His tone was matter-of-fact, like it had been since Shay's ma's funeral, but Shay still couldn't get used to it. It was like Frank had shut the door on grief so absolutely that missing Shay's mother had become a casual conversation. *What do you want from him? Tears and hysterics every time you speak?*

Shay shuddered. Fuck no. His father had always been his rock, even when his life took turns Frank didn't truly understand.

Crying didn't make a man weak, but Shay was weak enough to be glad it had never happened.

"So where are you off to now?" Frank pressed when Shay failed to fill the gap. "I told Sheila next door you were in Scotland, but I got that wrong, didn't I?"

"I called you from Newcastle last night."

"Ah, that's right. You're moving around so much I get confused."

"Well, I'm heading to Sunderland now, so you can tell her that when you next see her."

Shay would bet his banjo that would happen sooner rather than later. Frank mentioned Sheila every time they spoke, and Shay was okay with that. His father—God willing—had decades left to live. Shay didn't want him to be on his own.

Frank said something. Shay snapped back into the present. "Hmm?"

"I said, where are you at with that family tree thing? I couldn't make head or tail of the stuff you sent me on that Anna girl. She sounds bonkers."

"She wasn't bonkers. Just different."

"Aye, well that makes sense if you have her blood, then, eh?"

Warmth flooded Shay's chest. He was so lucky to have a father who thought like Frank. Who had nothing invested in Shay's life but love and support. Not everyone had that—hell, half the band didn't have it. "I don't know what's coming up next, just that Ollie is taking me somewhere tomorrow to show me something."

"Ollie?"

"The bloke from Sky."

"Oh aye. You've mentioned him before."

"Have I?"

"Every time we speak, son."

Oops. "So why didn't you know who he was?"

"Because you call him Ollie, don't ya? Not the bloke from Sky. How am I supposed to keep up?"

Frank Maloney was sharp as a tack. If Shay had mentioned Ollie every time they'd spoken since he'd left Derby, then Shay was willing to risk another bet on him knowing why. "Don't start."

"Not starting anything. Just pleased you're having fun. How long have you got left?"

Shay did a quick mental count up. "Two weeks, give or take," he said faintly. "Shit. It's gone so fast."

Frank shouted to one of the dogs. Shay pictured him tramping around the fields, his beloved deerhounds racing ahead of him, all long legs and silver fur. He *missed* him, but the prospect of the tour ending was something he couldn't quite contemplate.

Ollie would go back to London, and Shay would go wherever this crazy life took him. He wasn't ready for that.

He wasn't ready for this to end.

CHAPTER FIFTEEN

OLLIE PARKED the van at the venue and tossed the keys to Fred and Khalid—the two fresh roadies who didn't drink or smoke and had zero interest in partying. Corina had hired them on the promise that they would spend every night they weren't working watching football in the lounge of whatever hotel she was hiding out in. They were happy, the band was happy, and Corina... wasn't as pissed off as usual.

Winner.

Ollie grabbed his laptop and camera gear and automatically glanced around for Shay. As luck would have it, he stepped off the bus right into Ollie's path.

"Hey."

Shay's face was half-hidden by his hat and hair. "Hey, yourself. Everything okay?"

"Yup." Ollie resisted the urge to tip Shay's fedora back, cup his face in his palm, and rub his thumb over Shay's delicate cheekbone. The whole bus knew he'd spent the last couple of nights in Shay's bed—perhaps they even knew that first night had been more than a platonic knockout—but they didn't need to see him lose himself in Shay's lovely face. Fuck, no one needed to see that. "I've got to go find some Wi-Fi for a conference call. If I text you an address, can you meet me around four?"

"I thought we were meeting at two?"

"We were, but some work shit has come up."

"You're not in trouble for driving the van, are you?"

Ollie winced. "Not that I know of, but I can probably swing that because I'd be on the bus anyway."

"Don't get in trouble for us."

I'd get in trouble for you every day. "I won't." Ollie tried for a grin and then walked away, heart pounding.

It was true that he had a conference call to deal with, but it was more than that. Since the night he'd let his guts spill in Shay's bed, he'd felt strange. Not bad, but not good, and he needed some space to figure it out—even if it was just a few hours.

He'd never know what had possessed him to do it. Perhaps it was the acceptance he'd seen in Shay's eyes ever since. Maybe it had always been there but was amplified now that Ollie had taken a tiny step off the edge of the world. Either way, Ollie needed an hour, or three, to get his head around something he'd never expected to contemplate when he'd taken this job.

The venue the band were playing wasn't far from the maritime heritage site where Ollie planned to meet Shay, but he set off in the opposite direction and found a quiet pub to set up his makeshift office. Amir called dead on two o'clock. They reviewed the footage Ollie had produced so far.

"Wow." Amir whistled when the last frame played out. "He's got fantastic presence. You could almost convince me he didn't know the camera was there."

Ollie started to scoff, but then it occurred to him that Amir was halfway right. Shay obviously knew the camera was in the room with him, but he never looked at it. Never changed his behaviour, no matter how close it came to him. For the entire segment, Shay gave the subject matter his complete attention. And it was such a *Shay* thing to do. "He's, uh, easy to work with."

"I'll bet. My wife loves him."

Ollie bristled. "That's not what I meant."

After a long pause, Amir cleared his throat. "I didn't mean

anything, Ollie. Just that Fatima has been listening to the band with the kids."

Jesus-fucking-Christ. "I know. Sorry. Tour life is wearing me out."

"Understandable. We can probably pull you off early if it's getting too much. Make some arrangements to film a couple of segments at a later time. I know I pushed you to join the tour, but I was hoping you'd enjoy being out of London for a while."

"I am enjoying it." And Ollie realised with a start that he genuinely was. Travelling was tough, and he wasn't used to having people up in his face all the time, but as the long days had turned into weeks, he'd come to appreciate the camaraderie and friendship. How he was never alone unless he truly wanted to be.

"Fair enough," Amir said when Ollie failed to follow up. "We'll let it roll for now, but if you change your mind, let me know. I'll take care of it for you."

Ollie barely heard him.

Barely heard himself thank Amir and end the call. He set the phone down on the table and clicked randomly on his laptop screen, but his gaze was unseeing, his mind elsewhere. He pictured himself leaving the tour early, getting off the bus in London and going back to his old life while Shay and the band drove away. His eyes stung. *I don't want to go home.*

The realisation was startling, but undeniable. The clusterfuck rollercoaster he'd tumbled into the moment he'd met Shay was hurtling towards a destination unknown, but Ollie didn't want to get off.

Not yet.

Shay turned a slow circle in the huge dockyard. "Ships?"

"That's right." Ollie panned the gimbal in a wide shot, then settled on Shay. "What do you know about the year 1912?"

"Um… the Titanic sank?"

"Correct, and ten points for being topical. What about 1943?"

"Fuck all."

"Language."

"Shit, I mean, not much."

Ollie laughed. "Don't worry, I can edit that out." He killed the shot and hefted the gimbal onto his shoulder. "Come with me."

He led Shay into the heritage centre. A special room had been reserved for them in the basement. Safely inside, and surrounded by all the builder's tea and Gregg's doughnuts they could possibly want, Ollie directed Shay to an armchair by the loaded bookshelves. He set the camera on the tripod, lined up the shot, and turned it on.

Then he perused the shelves until he found what he was looking for.

The thick book was covered in dust. It misted the air as Ollie dropped it on the small table, and Shay waved his hand to dispel it. "So this is about ships?"

"Ship *building*, to be precise," Ollie corrected. "They've been building ships around here since 1346."

"The Titanic wasn't built here, was it?"

"Nothing about today has anything to do with the Titanic."

Shay pulled a face. "Shame. I was hoping I could pretend I was clever because I've seen the film."

God, he was cute. Ollie cleared his throat. "Anyway, so I only found out about who I'm going to show you today by accident. I was looking to see if you had any relatives who'd fought in the Second World War, and this person came up."

"They weren't a soldier then?"

"Nope."

"So he was a ship builder?"

"Joyce King, née Kasperson, to be exact." Ollie opened the book and tapped on a page. "*She*, my friend, was your great-great-grandmother."

Shay stared at the book, eyes wide, and Ollie stared at him. Research-wise, he'd struck gold when he'd dug into Shay's rich family history, but in real life, there was nothing more colourful than the wonder in his eyes as Ollie revealed it to him, piece by piece.

"Which side is she from?"

"Your mother's."

"Of course…. Kaspersen. That's the Danish side, right?"

"Yes. Rudolph was her grandfather, though her mother was English. Her husband too, so the Danish part is slowly fading at this point."

Shay nodded and went back to studying the photograph. It was better quality than any images Ollie had shown him so far, and he wondered if Shay was starting to see himself in body as well as spirit. "It's so strange," Shay said. "I feel like I'm on the ceiling, looking down on this happening to someone else."

Ollie had felt the same many times over the last few years. His hands twitched to reach for Shay, but the amount of overfamiliarity he already had to cut from existing footage kept him still. "I can't imagine how this feels for you, especially when you had no idea any of these people existed. It's different when you're half-aware that you had relatives who lived extraordinary lives. You expect the twists and turns, even if you don't know where they'll be."

Shay traced the text below the photograph of Joyce King with his finger. "Tell me about her?"

Ollie nodded. He had little to offer Shay in every other facet of their relationship, but he could do this. "Well, it all starts and ends in Sunderland. In 1938, it was the biggest shipbuilding town in the world. That year, 169,000 tons were produced here."

"Is that a lot?"

Ollie shot Shay an idiot scowl the camera wouldn't pick up. "It's a lot, and Joyce's entire family were involved with it—her father, uncles, brothers… her husband."

"Husband? So he was my great-great-grandfather?"

"Not exactly. But we'll get to that."

Shay's face was alive with curiosity, from his wide, blazing eyes, to his lip caught in his teeth. He tapped the book page. "Go on."

"In 1939," Ollie said, "war broke out. Joyce's husband was old enough to avoid the first waves of conscriptions, but he shipped out in 1940, and by then, much of Sunderland's male shipbuilding force had already gone. And it was the worst possible timing for the town. The war brought a huge boost in demand, so to keep up, the women stepped in. Turn the page."

Shay obeyed, and a double-paged photograph of women in the shipyards greeted him. "Wow. So many of them."

"They had a lot to do." Ollie turned another page. "And they weren't just building new ships. They were repairing warships and merchant boats that had already been damaged by U-boat attacks. I had a figure somewhere for the tonnage they produced in 1941, but I've lost it."

Shay chuckled softly. "It's probably in your bunk. I don't know how you live in such chaos."

"I don't spend much time there, in case you hadn't noticed."

Shay glanced up from the book. His gaze was charged with a new kind of heat. Or maybe it wasn't new at all. Whatever. Ollie was lost in it for a moment so protracted he'd need a sledge-hammer to edit it out.

"Um… anyway." Ollie fought to compose himself. Failed as Shay's long leg wrapped around his like a snake. A grin burst out of him before he could catch it. "Stop it. You make me insane."

"No, I make you smile. One day you'll realise that's not a bad thing."

"I already—fuck. Can we get this shit done? I can tell you how beautiful you are later."

Shay stared.

Ollie reached under the table and squeezed his lean, unyielding thigh. "Please?"

Heartbeats flowed between them. Then Shay blinked and turned back to the book. "So ships, yeah?"

Ollie sniggered and left his hand where it was.

<h1 style="text-align:center">CHAPTER SIXTEEN</h1>

SHAY LINKED his arm with Ollie's as they strolled by the waterside. They'd returned Ollie's laptop and camera gear to the bus and found no one around, so they'd snuck away again for a quick walk before Shay was due at soundcheck. "I can't believe my great-great-grandmother was involved in such a love triangle."

Ollie hummed. He hadn't resisted when Shay had taken his left arm, but the ripple of tension in him was hard to miss. "It actually wasn't that unusual in those days. Men were mistakenly reported dead quite frequently, and what were the women left behind supposed to do? Mourn forever?"

"I think my dad has a girlfriend."

"That's nice."

"It is. He won't tell me, though. I reckon he's worried I'll think it's too soon."

"Do you?"

"Nah. My mum will be dead forever. There's no need for him to be lonely." Shay kicked a rock. "I still can't believe my great-great-grandfather was an American GI."

"You're quite a mix, eh?"

"Yeah. It's weird. I'd never considered so many places could make up one person, and there's more to come, isn't there?"

"There is."

Shay shook his head. "I feel like a trifle."

"Fruity?"

"Nah. All mixed up."

Ollie laughed. Not for the first time, it took Shay to another planet. "I think that's a line from *Birds of a Feather*," Ollie said.

Shay resisted the urge to nudge him. "Sue me."

"Are you rich?"

"Only in things that matter."

Ollie hummed again, but it was distant this time, and Shay let him be. This quiet time was sacred, and despite spending the last two nights wrapped up in each other, he couldn't quite believe it was real.

"I'm sorry, you know," Ollie said after a while.

"What for?"

Ollie shrugged. "For dropping my shit on you in the middle of the night. I didn't mean to."

"Didn't mean to do it then, or didn't mean to do it at all?"

"Both. Neither. I don't know. I was having a bit of a headfuck about it earlier, but then I started imagining how it would be if we'd never met, and I figured that would be worse."

"I think that's the nicest thing you've ever said to me."

Ollie snorted. "Then I need to try a bit harder. If it's any consolation, I feel nice things when you're around."

Shay stopped walking. "What are we doing?"

"Huh?" Ollie trailed to a stop too. "What do you mean?"

"Don't be obtuse, Ollie."

"Obtuse?"

"Yeah. I know big words too."

"It's six letters long."

"Don't be a twat. I'm not asking for declarations here, mate. I just need to know—"

"Need to know what?" Ollie snapped as shadows descended on his gorgeous face like nightmares falling from the sky. "Every fault and flaw before you decide if I'm worth the hassle? Because I can save us both the trouble by confirming I'm really fucking not."

"Ollie—"

"Don't. Just—" Ollie tore his arm free and threw up his arms as if to shove Shay back from him. "Just don't bother. I've told you before… everything you can't see is a mess, and that's not going to change. Besides, the tour ends in two weeks. What the fuck do you think is going to happen next?"

He was flushed by the time he'd finished his expletive-heavy rant, and his accent had thickened to the point where Shay feared for a moment that he barely recognised him. Hurt lashed his heart, and his eyes grew damply hot. Ollie was going to walk away from him, again, and by doing so would prove himself right because nothing would change.

No.

Shay made a grab for Ollie. Ollie stepped away. Shay reached for him again, and Ollie backed himself against a tree, the light impact unnaturally loud on the quiet waterside. He sucked in a shaky breath. His cheeks were still stained pink from the tirade that had come from somewhere Shay had never seen, but his eyes were different now. Distant. Lost. But there was something else too. Something that frightened Shay more than anything.

Defeat.

"Ollie."

"*Shay.*" Ollie closed his eyes. He balled his hands into fists, and he seemed to shrink against the bark as though that would hide him from Shay… and from the rest of the world. "I can't do this."

"I'm not asking you to do anything."

"But you will."

"How do you know?"

Silence, but it wasn't silent. Shay stepped impossibly closer to Ollie, and the thunder in his ears was too loud to be his heart beating alone. He gripped Ollie's wrists, his fingers sliding under Ollie's coat and then his ever-present hoodie. Ollie's breath caught, but he didn't wrench his arms free.

Emboldened, Shay stretched his fingers as far as they'd go, ghosting over smooth warmth until the landscape changed. His fingertips found raised flesh and ruined skin. Found heartache and pain. Ollie's pain. A hot trickle carved its way down Shay's face. A single tear dripped onto Ollie's exposed wrist, but he still didn't open his eyes.

Shay stilled his fingers and kissed Ollie's jaw. He pressed his cheek against Ollie's and then laid a palm over his heart, as if he could slow it down by wordlessly asking. "Life goes on, Ollie," he whispered. "Even when you've given up living."

Predictably, Ollie said nothing, and for once Shay was glad of it.

———

SHAY HEFTED Larry's bass drum up the steps to the stage. The band were throwing everything at tonight's show, and despite Fred and Khalid's best efforts, even with Ollie's help, everyone had to pitch in.

It was hard work, and Shay was glad of the distraction. It had been two days since they'd left Sunderland, and two days since he'd shared anything more than benign conversation with Ollie. Were it not for the note Ollie had left tucked into Shay's favourite lyric book, he'd have lost his damn mind.

Give me time.

From anyone else, it might not have meant much, but from Ollie, it meant everything, even if time was in short supply. They were in Cardiff now, with less than a fortnight left on the tour, and Ollie's words echoed ominously in his head every time he found himself unoccupied. *"What the fuck do you think is going to happen next?"*

Something. Everything. Shay wished he'd had the balls to say so instead of shoving his hands up Ollie's sleeves and trying to force the one thing Ollie had explicitly promised would never happen.

He's never even shown his mum.

That bothered Shay almost more than anything else.

Almost because Shay was struggling to picture a reality that didn't include building on the inferno Ollie lit inside him with every kiss, and he felt like shit for it.

And yet he couldn't stop.

He dragged the bass drum into position. In his peripheral vision, he was aware of Ollie climbing the steps on the right-hand side of the stage, loaded down by a guitar and a case containing Shay's collection of woodwind instruments. He was wearing his battered leather jacket, his aviator shades still in place from the long drive down from Sunderland. The huge Cardiff venue faded away. To Shay, Ollie seemed to be on the wrong side of the road, where they were destined to pass like ships in the night.

Ollie sensed Shay's gaze on him and smiled. Shay smiled back, but with Ollie sleeping in his own bunk again, it wasn't nearly enough.

"Where do you want these?"

Shay jumped. Somehow Ollie had come up on him in three seconds flat. "What?"

"Your guitar and whatever's in this." Ollie held up the woodwind case.

Shay pointed at the loose stage position he usually began every show with. It wasn't set in stone, but he knew Ollie well enough to guess he wouldn't have the patience for vague answers right now. Not when he seemed to be coordinating the entire gig setup while Shay angsted himself into a hypo. *Dammit.*

Aware there was little time before soundcheck, Shay left the stage and found some privacy to get himself together. He ate enough to keep him going well into the evening, calculated his insulin dose, and shot it into his abdomen.

He packed his kit away and found a sink to wash his hands. The finger he'd drawn blood from throbbed. Somehow he'd lost the knack for testing himself without pain, and it wasn't hard to trace it back to the few times Ollie had done it for him. His gentle touch had eclipsed anything Shay could do for himself, and now every jab in his fingertip felt like a fucking snakebite.

Drama queen. But still.

Shay returned to the stage. It was deserted—the rest of the

band likely doing the same as him, without the minuscule blood-bath. He climbed the steps and drifted to the middle of the stage. The venue was the biggest they'd played so far—the biggest they'd *ever* played—and Shay couldn't deny he was nervous. Intimate gigs were his jam, or storming smaller venues with a riotous set, boots stomping, beer flying all over the place. With its rows and rows of stadium-style seats and contained standing area at the front, the Cardiff venue was a different league. A step up. What if they couldn't find the magic that had propelled them this far? What if they weren't ready?

Breathing deeply, Shay lay down on the stage. The weathered wood felt good against his back, and he closed his eyes. Some days he thought he could pinpoint the exact moment Ollie had taken over his every errant thought. Others, he wasn't altogether sure how he'd come to be on the brink of the biggest gig of his life with so many other things on his mind.

Someone lay down beside him. Before the tour it would've been Jumbo. Now it was Ollie, the warmth of his body torturously close, but not close enough.

Shay didn't open his eyes, and Ollie didn't speak. For long minutes they lay in their own brand of typical silence, both soothing and frightening… and utterly consuming.

Then Ollie sighed. "I can leave, you know."

"What?"

"The tour. If I'm making things hard for you."

Shay opened his eyes and rose slightly, propping himself up on one elbow. "Why would I want you to leave?"

"I just said why." Ollie stared up at him. His eyes seemed darker than usual. "All the guys are worried about how moody you are, and I'm thinking it's probably my fault."

"Because the world revolves around you?"

"No, because I'm the only thing that's different from the last time you went on tour."

"We don't even play the same show twice. How the fuck do you figure this tour is a carbon copy of the last one? That's insane."

"I meant emotionally, not literally."

"Oh. Well, you're still wrong."

Ollie smirked faintly. "I like being wrong."

"Why?"

"Because I'm a pessimist."

"Have you always been?"

"No."

"Then you have plenty of time to change back."

Ollie opened his mouth to speak. Shay silenced him with the first kiss they'd shared in days. Then he lay back down with his head on Ollie's chest and stayed there until the world moved on.

CHAPTER SEVENTEEN

CARDIFF WAS wild. Smuggler's Beat played three shows, each one more stomping than the last, and by the time they finished, the entire cast and crew were wiped out. Only Ollie and Corina seemed unaffected by exhaustion, and that, Ollie mused, was likely because neither one of them slept much anyway.

"Vampires," Ben muttered when he got up for a piss one night to find them hunched over coffee and laptops.

Ollie flipped him off. Corina ignored him, not looking up from her work until he was safely snoring in his bed again. "How come you're not sleeping with Shay anymore?"

"Excuse me?"

"You heard. Don't be coy, Ollie. There's nowhere to hide on a tour like this."

"You spend plenty of time hiding in hotels."

"Only because sharing my bedroom with six other people gets on my nerves. You think I'm a cow already? Wait until I've spent a solid week with this lot."

Ollie had a certain sympathy for her there, but where *he* slept at night was none of her business, though he wasn't daft enough to tell her so. He went with the other convenient truth. "I was never sleeping with him. It isn't like that."

Corina returned her gaze to her laptop screen. "I don't believe you. The technicalities aren't important, but I can't imagine anyone ever spending the night with Shay and it 'not being like that.' That kid is beautiful."

"I know that."

"So why are you pretending it doesn't matter?"

The Ollie who'd joined the tour a few weeks ago would've told her to fuck right off, but something had shifted in him the last few days, and he wanted to understand as much as Corina did. More. "I'm not pretending it doesn't matter, it's just… hard, when there's no privacy and everyone's so busy and knackered. Nothing feels real."

"Never does on tour." Corina tapped a few keys on her laptop, her ever-present frown turning thoughtful. "Do you think you'll stay in touch when this is all over?"

Ollie swallowed thickly, unwilling to admit how many times he'd pictured the end of the tour, of waving goodbye to the bus—to Shay—and returning to his old life like nothing had happened. As though he was the same person he'd been before he met Shay, and it wouldn't rip him in two to leave him. "I hope so. He, um, gets me, and I'm starting to appreciate that."

"You know, there's a couple of rest days coming up after the London shows before we head up to Leeds for the final dates."

Ollie nodded. He'd been planning on going home and recharging before filming the final scenes of Shay's documentary.

"I was planning on sending Shay home to Derby," Corina continued, "rather than putting him in the hotel with the others. He's wiped out, and I think he could do with a break."

"Uh-huh."

"So…."

"So what?"

"Why don't you take him back to your place for a few days?"

Ollie dragged the element he was working on into the wrong place and dropped it there, ruining an hour's worth of editing. "Shit."

"It's that horrifying?"

"No, not that. Fuck. Sorry." Ollie gave up and closed his laptop. "You want me to what?"

"It's not about what I want."

"I don't understand."

Corina sighed. "Look, I'm not going to pretend I have the first clue what's going on with you and him, but take it from me, whatever it is, you'll never be able to see it clearly while you're trapped on a cramped bus with an audience and while he's working so much. Get away from it all, even if it's just twenty-four hours. It'll be worth so much more than a month spent like this."

She waved a hand around, then turned back to her laptop as though she hadn't flayed herself open wide enough for Ollie to see that her clipped, impatient advice came from a place of painful personal experience.

Ollie stared at the side of her head, panic and excitement sluicing through him in equal measure. Home was a sanctuary, where he'd always been deliberately and wonderfully alone. Where he'd spent a year stumbling around with his skin hanging off and his brain still stuck in the back of that damn burning car. The thought of taking Shay there seemed somehow shameful, as though Shay would see the worst of Ollie simply by walking through the door, but at the same time, he pictured Shay everywhere in his tiny one-bedroom flat—curled up on his couch, leaning in the kitchen doorway, asleep in his bed.

I want that.

"Where are we?"

Ollie glanced down at Shay. "Southampton. We drove here after the show last night, remember?"

Shay gazed up at him, sleep addled and confused. "We're not in Bristol anymore?"

"Nope. And we were there less than twelve hours. It's okay not to recall much of it."

Shay rolled over and dropped his head in Ollie's lap, a quiet groan escaping him. Ollie rubbed the back of his neck and glanced around for Shay's medical bag. Though Shay had stumbled off stage like a zombie the night before, he'd been in good shape, blood-sugar–wise. Hopefully he'd be able to sleep a bit longer.

He found the bag and tested Shay's blood as unobtrusively as possible, relieved to find it was in the range where Shay had assured him he didn't have to do anything for a while. Shay didn't move. He wasn't asleep, Ollie could tell, but clearly had zero interest in being awake.

Ollie let him be. The last few days had been insanely busy, five shows, two cities, and barely enough time to breathe, let alone squeeze in the filming that was the only reason they'd ever met. But somehow, they'd managed it.

"So I'm Russian?"

Ollie shook his head. "No. This bit of Europe isn't part of Russia anymore."

"Fuck's sake." Shay groaned and banged his head on the table. "Why don't I know this shit?"

"Because it's never been relevant until now?"

"That's a crap excuse for ignorance."

"But still… more musicians, Shay. How cool is that?"

Ollie tipped his head back and closed his eyes, warmth filling his chest as he recalled how Shay had smiled at him then, hazel eyes filled with wonder and… something else Ollie had yet to decipher. It had been nice to show Shay that his past contained people who had simply lived, the way Shay did, for nothing but music and love. Ollie had clung to Shay's smile for the rest of that day.

He wished it were still that day. They had one segment left to film up north, in Leeds, and he wasn't sure how Shay would react to what he'd discover there, so he held on to the joy they'd found in Bristol, kept it close, and made the most of Shay curled up in his lap.

Too soon, though, it was time for Shay to wake up and get to work. Smuggler's Beat were playing three back-to-back shows in

Southampton and then swinging into Portsmouth for one more before they made the journey to London.

London. Ollie's heart skipped a beat. He still hadn't asked Shay to come home with him. After the initial giddiness Corina's suggestion had left him with, reality had set in, soaking through his mood like heavy rain on sand. That morning, he'd left the bus before Shay had woken up, only to return that night and crawl into his bed. And skulk back to his own the next night. Rinse and repeat. *Man, I'm so fucked up.* And he still wanted Shay to come home with him.

More than anything in the world.

"Ollie?"

"Hmm?"

Shay frowned and then smiled and then frowned again. "I'm so fucking tired."

"I know." Ollie tucked a stray lock of hair behind Shay's ear. "You want me to bring you breakfast in bed?"

"Breakfast?"

"Yes, mate. It's still morning."

Shay nodded slowly. "I keep waking up with you and wondering if you're real."

Guilt flared in Ollie's gut. "Because I'm creeping in and out of your bed like a—"

Shay covered Ollie's mouth with his hand. "Don't finish that sentence."

Ollie waited a beat, then pushed Shay's hand aside. "Bad jokes aside, I'm sorry."

"Why?"

"Because I want to sleep in your bed all the time, and I keep making you think that I don't."

"I know you want to sleep with me, Ollie, in the literal sense, at least."

"You do?"

Shay rolled out of Ollie's lap. "Yes. If I didn't, it wouldn't happen."

Ollie had no clue what that meant, and, as was typical in

conversations like this with Shay, his loose tongue was handicapped by the lump in his throat. He wanted to apologise again, but something in Shay's gaze stopped him. Instead, he made himself useful and sloped off to get breakfast.

Jumbo helped himself to Ollie's cigarettes. "Why don't you come to rehearsals, seeing as you've got nothing to do?"

"What makes you think I've got nothing to do?"

"Dude, you've been sitting in front of that laptop for an hour, and you haven't typed your password in yet."

Fuck. Ollie's fingers twitched to tap in his login details and give Jumbo a reason to sod off already, but his heart wasn't in it. He shut the laptop with a bang. "Whatever. Give me my fags back."

Jumbo returned the pack, minus a couple of smokes—one for him, one for Ben. Somehow, Ollie had become the band's tobacco supplier, roadie, *and* the worst groupie in the world. "So...," Jumbo said. "Are you coming to rehearsals, or what?"

"What do you care?"

"I'm hung-over, man. I don't think I can get through a four-hour session without knowing I've got a wingman to keep me in coffee and smokes."

Ollie treated Jumbo to his best dead-eyed stare. "I have never, and will never be, your wingman, you fucking goon."

"Worth a try, though, eh?"

It really wasn't, and Ollie was bemused by Jumbo's claim to be hung-over when Corina had herded the band onto the bus the minute their gear had been packed away, but Jumbo was apparently unaffected by Ollie's acerbic tongue. He flashed a lazy wink and meandered off the bus.

Restlessness built in Ollie as he watched Jumbo zigzag the car park before he seemed to figure what direction he was supposed to be headed. So far, Ollie had steered clear of rehearsals and soundchecks, only seeing Smuggler's Beat play during their shows or the spontaneous jam sessions they fell into at random moments on any given day. And he happened to know that rehearsing was among Shay's least favourite things to do. Add in the fact that Ollie was likely irritating the fuck out of him right now, showing up seemed like a dick move.

But staying away was impossible. Ollie was shit at verbalising how Shay consumed him, but his brain had no problem interpreting the live wires of emotion that zapped through him in conflicting directions. Ollie packed his laptop away and fished his camera out of his kit bag. Focusing on film, he'd taken no still photographs for weeks—unheard of when he was in London. He attached the flash and his favourite lens to his camera and looped the strap over his head. The weight of the camera around his neck grounded him a little, and he left the bus before the ever-present devil on his shoulder got the better of him.

The Southampton venue was smaller than Bristol and Cardiff —the seats and standing areas packed enough to feel intimate when it was full the brim later. Which it would be; every show since Glasgow had sold out.

Ollie stood at the back and observed the band while he considered various shots. As ever, there seemed to be no coherence in whatever it was the band were trying to do. Ben was on his phone, while Jumbo appeared to be asleep. Mara sat at the piano, and Larry was tapping out a beat completely unrelated to the Rachmaninov she was playing. Ollie wished he'd brought his video gear after all. Then his gaze landed on Shay, who was clearly in a world of his own, lost in a song only he could hear.

God, he was beautiful.

Ollie moved silently through the rows of seats, watching through the lens of his camera as Shay played his penny whistle in a haunting tune that seemed almost to be carried in the wind to Ollie's ears. It was ethereal, but *so Shay* at the same time, and déjà vu hit Ollie in waves. Had he heard this song before or simply been enraptured by Shay so often he couldn't tell reality from dreams?

Either way, Ollie was again enchanted. He slipped into the

shadows of the standing area and snapped shots of Shay as he picked up the melody. In a wider shot, Ollie caught Larry observing Shay, too, and tracked him as he brought a small drum across the stage to sit by Shay. Ben soon followed, and then Mara brought an instrument Ollie didn't recognise. The song built in tempo and intensity until it bore all the hallmarks of a Smuggler's Beat classic, but with the lyrics coming from Shay's penny whistle.

It was… something else, and Ollie realised with a start that it *was* a scene he'd seen play out before, but it seemed different this time—for him and for Shay.

He snatched a dozen shots before he finally lowered the camera to find Shay staring at him, head tilted sideways.

"How long have you been there?" Shay called.

Ollie ventured closer to the stage. "Long enough. I like that song. Is it new?"

Shay shrugged. "We just made it up, so I guess so, but it didn't feel that way."

"It reminded me of the Lithuanian folk stuff I gave you."

Comprehension coloured Shay's features. "*That's* where it came from. It's been bugging me for days."

"Really?"

"Yes… don't look at me like I'm crazy. I can't help it."

"I don't think you're crazy, mate. Even if I did, I'd be a hypocrite."

That earned Ollie a crinkled frown, but it was fleeting. Shay had other things on his mind, and he played another series of notes on his whistle that sounded Lithuanian in origin but brighter and faster than the last song.

The rest of the band picked it up immediately, and Ollie tapped his foot too. Larry offered him a drum, but Ollie shook his head and backed away. It had been a *long* time since he'd picked up an instrument of any kind, and he wasn't about to embarrass himself in front of a group of people who already seemed to know him better than he sometimes knew himself.

He retreated to the back of the standing area and sat down on the cold floor. His camera provided a buffer between him and Shay, but only until he started clicking through the photos he'd taken. *Jesus. Why have I waited so long to shoot him?* On film, Shay had a presence that drew the eye and sucked up space, but in a still photograph he was so much more—even in the shots that hadn't captured his face. Ollie studied an image of Shay's fingertips dancing on the penny whistle. Without the music it told a story of its own, and Ollie would've known the hands were Shay's if someone had shown it to him.

The band moved on to playing crowd-pleasers and album tracks. Ollie listened for a while longer, but the Lithuanian vibe Shay had brought to the table earlier stuck with him. Though the songs Ollie had heard were cracking, he'd sensed Shay's frustration with them. They were part of him, but not the whole of him, and the mirror of what they were doing on film wouldn't leave Ollie alone.

He snuck out of the venue and went back to the bus. Online, he found the roots of something that might help, and he spent the rest of the day chasing the storm.

SHAY HELD the strange wooden instrument up to the light. "What is it?"

From his position on the floor below the stage, Ollie shook his head. "I'm not going to tell you, and I don't want you to look it up, okay? Just keep it around for a while. See if it speaks to you."

"You're such a weirdo."

"You like that shit."

Shay couldn't deny it. Ollie was strange about lots of things—mainly himself—but when he did stuff like this, Shay fell for him a little bit harder. *This is dangerous.* But it was too late to get off that particular train, so Shay merely lay down on the stage, belly to the wood, and leaned down to kiss Ollie on the lips, not giving a single fuck who saw them.

Ollie blinked, clearly surprised, but Shay didn't much care about that either. They'd shared a bed for four nights in a row now —their longest stretch yet—and Shay had kissed Ollie last night, too, and snuck his hands under Ollie's ever-present hoodie. Ollie hadn't flinched. Much. That had to count for something, right?

PDA done, Shay took the instrument back to the band. Only Mara's face held a flicker of recognition, but Shay shook his head. "Don't tell me what it is. It's part of the other, uh, thing."

Mara raised a perfect brow. "How are you going to learn to play it if you don't know what it is?"

"I don't know if I'm meant to play it."

"If the boy gives it to you, it is for a reason, and what reason but to play it?"

Shay didn't have an answer for that, but he took Ollie at his word and set the instrument aside to study later when he had time. First, he had the Portsmouth show to play, and it was going to be *huge.* He could feel it in his bones.

He picked up his banjo and resumed tuning it. Ollie's presence made the back of his neck tingle, but he tried to ignore it. One more show, and then they had a few rest days before they hit London, and Shay couldn't wait. Corina had promised them hotel rooms and total freedom from tour commitments. Shay was hoping Ollie would spend that time with him. *We need it.* Shay didn't know much about him and Ollie, but he knew that. He flicked a glance over his shoulder, but Ollie was gone.

Dammit. Shay's heart sank, though he couldn't say why. Ollie had been to every show in Southampton and had given no indication that he wouldn't be at this one, but Shay felt his absence like a kick to the guts all the same. *And you call him a weirdo....*

HOURS LATER, the gig played out. Sweat soaked Shay's back, and he raised his banjo to the roof, taking a final bow, his chest heaving with the exertion of their second encore. It was fucking magic, and for the first time in their latest run of shows, he remembered why they did this. He might not have known where his blood came from, but he knew what made it sing.

Ollie's grinning face in the crowd was the icing on the cake.

The band trooped offstage. Shay jumped down the steps, sweat cooling as he left the heat of the crowd behind. Corina handed him a towel and a bottle of something cold and wet. He took it gratefully and tipped it down his throat, relaxing as it eased the dry mouth he'd been plagued with for the last half of the show. "Thanks—"

But she'd already moved on.

Shay tossed the bottle in a nearby bin and looked around for Ollie. Couldn't find him. Irrational edginess threatened Shay's postgig glow. *Idiot. He was right there in the crowd five minutes ago.* Which meant it would take him a while to fight his way backstage, and by then, it would be time to take the stage apart and load the van. *Fuck, does this never end.*

Apparently not. Shay's prophecy played out. He eventually found Ollie at the back of the stage, unravelling a mess of cables and wires.

"How do you lot manage this when I plug them in all pretty and untangled?"

"Uh, blame Jumbo?" Shay shrugged. "I don't know."

Ollie grunted and turned back to his task. The odd irritation building in Shay's belly crept up another notch, and he stomped away without bothering to reply.

He busied himself boxing up the microphones and guitar pedals, studiously ignoring the bustle around him. His sudden bad mood bothered him. He'd jumped off stage on top of the world, and now it seemed as though he was sinking to the bottom like a foul-tempered child, and he didn't know why. He was thirsty too, so thirsty that the three bottles of water he downed didn't touch the sides and yet still had him having to piss every five minutes.

Brilliant.

"Shay?"

"What?"

Mara narrowed her eyes. "It's time to go."

"Go?"

"Yeah, numbnuts. We're driving to London tonight so we get an extra day off. It was your idea, remember?"

It rang a bell, but Mara was already walking away. Shay stared after her, trying to gather the threads of his exhaustion-addled mind, and then he gazed around the now-empty venue.

Somehow he'd missed everyone leaving. Including Ollie. *Fuck's sake.*

Shay gathered the boxes he'd meticulously packed and piled them up. He stood and bent to retrieve them, but his vision darkened and his legs wobbled. Cursing, he steadied himself on the stack of boxes and made an attempt at calculating everything he'd consumed that day and the insulin doses he'd taken to back it up, but his brain was too fuzzy.

He gave up and concentrated on getting out of the venue and to the van without dropping thousands of pounds worth of gear. But when he got to the carpark, he found only the bus waiting for him.

Smugs took the mic boxes from him and stashed them away. He paid little attention to Shay, but then, he rarely did. Bemused, Shay fished his phone from his pocket, but there was no message from Ollie, just the blank screen of a dead battery. Shay pocketed the phone, suddenly unsure of what he'd been looking for in the first place. His throat burned, and goddammit if he didn't need to piss again.

On the bus, he used the bathroom, then grabbed another Coke and some fruit to perk him up. He passed Larry in the aisle. "Where'd the van go?"

"London, I'd imagine, lad. It's where the rest of us are going."

The answer made perfect sense, but the notion that Ollie had left without saying goodbye made no sense at all, even though nothing about how he communicated with Shay ever did.

Shaking his head to clear it, Shay shuffled along until he got to his bunk and then collapsed on his bed. He kicked his boots off and instantly fell into a restless doze that seemed to go nowhere.

Desperate for rest, he groaned when he woke up a little while later. The bus was rumbling its way north to London. Shay gazed a moment at the motorway zipping by, then rolled over, gaze habitually drawn to Ollie's bunk. It was empty, of course, but something else made Shay sit up sharply. Beyond Ollie's absence, everything else was gone from his bed too—his camera, his laptop bag, the screwed-up pair of sweatpants he sometimes slept in.

Even the bed was made. If Shay hadn't known better, it would seem as though Ollie had never been there at all. *Jesus, he's gone.* Stomach roiling, Shay lay back down. The irrational anxiety he'd carried since the end of the show quickened his pulse, and cold sweat dampened his skin. He felt clammy and strange, and the worst kind of heat built in his gut until he knew with horrifying certainty that he was going to be sick.

Panicked, he rolled off his bed and landed in a heap on the aisle floor. He scrambled to his feet and lunged for the bathroom, making it just in time to lose the buckets of fluid he'd consumed before he fell asleep. It seemed to go on forever, and when it was over, he slumped on the floor, too scared to move in case it happened again.

"Shay?"

"Go away, Jumbo."

"Not likely, mate. You never let me kip on the floor, no matter how bladdered I am."

I'm not drunk. But nothing came out when Shay tried to speak. Strong hands gripped his arms and lifted him from the floor. Jumbo propped him up and propelled him to the nearest empty bunk—Ollie's naturally. *Fuck my life.*

Jumbo crouched in front of him, his usual asinine grin replaced by a worried frown. "Do you need a Lucozade or some shit?"

Shay thought hard. Somewhere beneath the haze of his Ollie woes and the nausea ripping through him, he knew something was wrong, and he needed to fix it before he lost the ability to think for himself. Lord knew, Shay had spent enough time in hospitals to know it wasn't an experience worth having.

He reached clumsily for Jumbo, who was on the phone, speaking too quietly for Shay to hear him.

Jumbo caught his hand. Said more words. Then hung up the phone. "I don't know what to do, Shay. Someone else is always around when this shit happens."

"Where is everyone?"

"They went to check in."

Check in. Shay turned the words over and realised with a start that the bus wasn't moving anymore. *What the fuck?* He looked out of the window to see a faceless underground car park, and his stomach lurched again.

There was zero chance of him making it to the bathroom this time. He croaked out a warning to Jumbo, who moved faster than his large frame usually allowed. An empty beer box appeared in front of Shay. He heaved into it, and a stabbing pain lanced through his abdomen. "Ow."

The box vanished, taking Jumbo with it. Shay groaned and fell back on the bed, slumping against pillows that should've smelled like Ollie, but didn't. "Where is he?"

Jumbo reappeared and thankfully seemed to know who Shay meant. "I don't know, mate. I called him, but his phone isn't connecting. Corina's on her way back."

Another groan escaped Shay. He didn't want Corina and her cold hands and good intentions; he wanted—he *needed*—Ollie. And he needed to be sick again.

He was on his third round of making Jumbo play dodge the vomit when Corina's sharp heels sounded on the steps to the bus. She pushed Jumbo aside and gripped Shay's chin, assessing him with the limited knowledge she'd gleaned from seeing Shay in messes like this before.

"Get his bag," she ordered Jumbo. "We need to test his glucose levels right now."

Corina pulled Shay's hand towards her.

A deep-rooted instinct he couldn't control made him rip it away. "No."

"Shay."

"*No.* I can do it myself—"

A new voice suddenly cloaked Shay, surrounding him, protecting him. Corina's chilled touch and Jumbo's bumbling ignorance disappeared. Warm hands eased under Shay's body, lifting him until he was halfway upright and cradled in Ollie's arms.

Troubled eyes searched Shay's face. "What's wrong, mate?"

I don't want to be your mate. Shay shook his head. "I don't know. I feel really bad."

"You want me to check your sugars?"

"Yeah."

Ollie moved like he'd done it a thousand times, not the handful of occasions he had over the last few weeks. A tiny jab into Shay's finger, and then it was over, for Shay at least.

He closed his eyes. The sickness was fading now. He had the stomach ache from hell, and all he wanted was to sleep.

"Shay." Ollie shook him gently. "Your blood sugar is really high. I've never seen it like this, and I don't know what to do."

"Does he need food?" Corina said from somewhere. "I've never seen it high either."

"No food… yet," Ollie said. "I think he needs insulin first, but I don't know how much."

Shay fought the fog in his brain. It had been months since he'd had a level high enough to put him on his arse. Diabetes manifested itself differently in everyone, even if it followed particular trends, and his worst moments had always been low. *Come on. You know what to do. You can fix this.*

God, he wanted to. Being in Ollie's arms was fucking amazing, but the prospect of chucking up on him, or worse, was horrifying enough to spur his sluggish brain into motion.

Ollie passed him his insulin kit. With Herculean effort, Shay studied the numbers and calculated the dose. Then Ollie took the pen from Shay's trembling hands and injected the insulin into Shay's abdomen.

It would take a little while to kick in, but the psychosomatic effect was instant. Shay melted against Ollie, willing the tremors wracking his body to fade as Ollie spoke quietly to whoever was close by. Shay didn't care. Somewhere beneath it all he was mortified that Ollie had seen him in such a mess again and furious that the condition he'd managed for most of his life had chosen *right now* to fuck him over. But beyond all that, he just needed Ollie.

Deft, gentle fingers pushed Shay's damp hair out of his face.

Ollie was smiling, though it didn't quite meet his eyes. "You doing okay down there?"

"Yeah."

"Good. Don't worry about anything, okay? I'm going to check your levels again in a little while, and then maybe you can eat something?"

"Okay."

"Tell me if you feel worse, though. I don't really know what I'm doing here. Only what Google told me when I looked it up a few weeks ago."

"That's cute."

"Shh. Don't tell anyone."

The exchange finished Shay off. He closed his eyes and let Ollie's soothing fingers lull him into the kind of doze he never wanted to wake up from if it meant Ollie would hold him like this forever. He was dimly aware of more sharp scratches on his fingertips, but he paid little attention to any of it until Ollie roused him sometime later.

"You should eat now," he said. "Your levels are starting to dip."

"Okay." Shay sat up and accepted a banana. "Where did everybody go?"

"Into the hotel. Jumbo was flapping, so Corina took him for a drink. She told me she'd murder me if I didn't take care of you, but it wasn't really necessary."

"Did you tell her that?"

Ollie looked up from studying the latest number on Shay's glucose metre. "Nah. I told her I'm taking you home."

CHAPTER NINETEEN

OLLIE HELPED Shay into the van and fastened his seat belt.

Shay rolled his eyes. "I could've done that."

"Yeah, well. Now you don't have to." Ollie shut the door before Shay could reply and hurried round to the driver's side.

He heaved himself up, fastened his own seat belt, then turned to Shay. "Ready? I mean, are you sure about this? I can walk you to your hotel room if you want."

"Shut up, Ollie."

Okay, then. Ollie fought a smile as he started the engine and eased the van out of the underground car park. Coming back to the bus to find Shay in such a mess had terrified him—*still* terrified him every time he took in Shay's pale skin and sunken eyes—but the sense that they were on the precipice of something wonderful was carrying him through. It wasn't the way he'd planned on asking Shay to come home with him, but it was what it was.

"I thought you'd gone."

"Hmm?" Ollie hung a left, then flicked a quick glance at Shay. "Gone where?"

"I don't know. Home? Away? Anywhere that wasn't near me?"

"I took Fred and Khalid to the train station. Why would you think I'd gone anywhere else?"

Shay shrugged listlessly. "Ask me later?"

Ollie had read online that funky blood sugar levels could provoke all kinds of emotional symptoms, but he'd have bet money that Shay's uncertainty stemmed from Ollie's yo-yo–like behaviour over the last few weeks. It was on the tip of his tongue to apologise for the dozenth time, but he didn't. What was the point? He could say what he liked. Only *doing* would fix this.

If it could be fixed at all.

Ollie drove into north London, keeping a sharp eye on Shay as they crossed the city. He dozed for a little while but seemed to perk up as they neared the nondescript block of flats Ollie called home.

"This is where you live?"

"Uh-huh." Ollie swung the van into a vacant space in the carpark and dug his spare permit out of his wallet. He slapped it on the dashboard and unbuckled his seat belt. "It's not much, but it's mine."

"You own it?"

"Yeah."

"Wow. You're rich."

"Not really, mate. You coming in?"

Shay nodded slowly.

Ollie slid out of the van, retrieved his camera gear and laptop from the back, checked the most expensive sound equipment was as secure as it was going to get, and locked up.

Shay opened the passenger door. Ollie caught him as he slid out and steadied him against the side of the van. "Give me your bag, I'll take it."

"I've got it."

"Shay—"

"Piss off."

Ollie let him be and took his arm instead, guiding him to the flat's revolving doors. In the lobby, he led him to the lift, and they rode to the twelfth floor. Ollie's flat was at the end of the corridor. He dropped his bags to wrestle with the front door and then shooed Shay inside.

He clicked the lights on, grateful that he employed a housekeeper to keep the place presentable even when he wasn't around. Shay liked things clean and tidy. Even himself. Especially himself. Ollie eyed him as he leaned in the living room doorway. With his tousled hair and rumpled clothes, drooping eyes and translucent skin, he didn't look like himself at all.

Ollie ditched his bags by the couch and, after a brief standoff, relieved Shay of his. "You wanna sit down?"

"Can I borrow your shower first?"

"Only if you put it back after."

"Twat."

"Yup. Come on. I'll get you some towels."

Ollie's flat was small and compact, and the last owners had kitted it out to look like an IKEA showroom. It made the place a little soulless, but the upside was it didn't take Ollie long to find everything Shay needed. "You going to be all right in there by yourself?"

Shay raised an eyebrow. "What if I wasn't? Would you get in with me?"

Yes. No. Maybe. Ollie rolled his eyes. "Just don't pass out in there, okay?"

Shay said nothing. He drifted into the bathroom and shut the door. Ollie winced at the harsh sound in the silent flat, then retreated to the kitchen to check the fridge. The shelves were pretty bare, but there were cheese, eggs, and milk. Bacon too. The housekeeper had left a loaf of bread on the counter, and Ollie had a squirrel stash of hot dinners in the freezer. They wouldn't starve, and more importantly, much of it was food Shay could actually eat.

Ollie pulled a Tupperware container out and dropped it in the sink to defrost for… *fuck, I don't even know what day it is anymore.* Not that it mattered. Corina had ordered him to deliver Shay back to her on Friday morning, preferably in one piece, and until

Thursday night rolled around, Ollie didn't give a fuck what day of the week it was.

The shower shut off. Ollie leaned on the counter and closed his eyes, willing himself to stay put and give Shay some privacy even as he pictured how Shay would look fresh out of the shower—damp hair, water still dripping down his alabaster skin.

"You have a guitar."

Ollie jumped and opened his eyes. Shay was leaning on the counter by the oven, an exact replica of the scene Ollie had just witnessed in his imagination, right down to the *Game of Thrones* pyjama bottoms he must've found in the bathroom. "Um. Yeah. I do."

"Do you play it?"

"No."

"But you did once?"

"Yes."

Shay sighed and folded his arms across his bare chest. "You know this is totally unbalanced, don't you?"

"What is?"

"That you've seen me at my absolute worst a hundred fucking times and you won't even tell me why you don't play your guitar anymore."

Dread bloomed in Ollie's veins, fresh and new and yet horribly familiar. "Why does it matter? I was never much good at it anyway."

"It's not about the fucking guitar!"

Shay's shout seemed to bounce off the kitchen cabinets and ricochet around Ollie's brain. It was too loud, and he searched for enough anger to defend himself with. To keep Shay out, if only for a little bit longer. "What do you want from me? A fucking strip-tease and a blow by blow account? What difference would it make? I'd still be me, and you'd still be you, and—"

"And what? You might be fucked in your own special way, but I have to do a damn equation every time I eat a sandwich, and do you know what happens when I don't?"

"I—"

"It was a rhetorical question, Ollie. You *do* know what happens to me when it all goes wrong, because you've seen it—you're looking at it right now. How would you feel if you couldn't? If you knew there was something about me that affected my whole life but I didn't trust you enough to let you see it?"

"Shay—"

"Don't." Shay cut Ollie off again. "I'm not even sure what I'm trying to say, I just can't handle the bullshit you throw up every time I ask the wrong fucking question. It hurts me, but it's gotta hurt you more, and I can't handle that. I don't want to make your life harder—"

Ollie pressed his lips to Shay's, silencing him, but for once not to shut him up. Each word dug into his hard-won shields, and finally they were starting to penetrate. He kissed Shay hard, and then softer, buying time as his entire axis seemed to shift.

He slid his palms down Shay's smooth torso, catching the lingering droplets of water, focusing on sensation, nothing more. Tunnel vision had always been his friend—as a child, as an adult, before and after the accident that had robbed him of the man he'd once been. He dropped his head on Shay's shoulder, counting Shay's breaths until it seemed that neither one of them was breathing anymore.

I can do this.

More than that. He wanted to, and the fear that had been his constant companion for so long was suddenly a dull roar he could face up to.

Maybe.

Perhaps.

Fuck it.

Ollie found Shay's wrist and guided it to the zip on his hoodie. Shay made a sound low in his throat but didn't protest as Ollie wrapped his fingers around it and forced him to draw it down.

The hoodie hung open. Ollie shrugged it away, leaving him with just a Bob Dylan T-shirt between the mess of his own torso and Shay's beautiful skin. *Take it off.*

No.

Yes.

Ollie raised his head, grasped the hem of his T-shirt, and slipped it over his head. It fell away like a ghost, leaving him bare to the weight of Shay's wide-eyed gaze and the cool stillness of the kitchen. A dozen cutting things he could've said danced through his mind, but he didn't say them. He didn't say anything. Couldn't while Shay was looking at him like that.

He's not horrified. Or maybe he was, and it didn't matter. Perhaps he felt sorry for Ollie, and that didn't matter either. Ollie reclaimed Shay's hand and placed it on the very thickest scars, the ones that had obscured his protruding ribs when he'd lost weight after the accident. "This is me, Shay," he whispered. "Now let it go… please."

He stepped back so Shay's hand slipped from him, taking with it the only kind of heat Ollie would ever need, and walked away.

OLLIE DIDN'T know where he was going until he found himself cloaked in the darkness of his bedroom, and he didn't know if Shay would follow him. But he did. Of course he fucking did. He followed him all the way to the window and stood behind him, so close that Ollie was sure he could hear Shay's heart beating.

Shay pressed his forehead between Ollie's shoulder blades. "I'm sorry I made you do that."

"Why?"

"I-I don't know? Because it wasn't what I meant about hiding?"

"I know it wasn't what you meant."

"So why did you do it?"

Slowly, Ollie turned around. Every part of him tingled, and he kissed Shay once, twice, three times. "Because of this. I knew it was real, but I had to be sure."

"You were worried I wouldn't want to kiss you after I saw you naked?"

"You haven't seen me naked."

Yet. Ridiculously, the word seemed to hang over them like a speech bubble. Shay raised his hands. Dropped them. Raised them again. "Can I touch you?"

Ollie shivered. "If you want."

"Of course I want to. I've done nothing but want you since we met."

"Why?"

"Shut *up*." Shay slid his arms around Ollie's waist, forcing them impossibly closer. "I care so much about you, okay? Even though you're a fucked up arsehole sometimes. It doesn't matter, Ollie. None of it does, for me, for you. Can't we just have this?"

He kissed Ollie, and their bodies moulded together, smooth and rough, dead flesh reborn as the spark between them flared into something Ollie couldn't control. Over and over, their lips met, hands roaming and starting new fires until Ollie didn't know where he ended and Shay began. Where the desolate moonscape of his ruined skin became the smooth planes that belonged to Shay.

Didn't know and didn't care. He would've kissed Shay forever if Shay hadn't swayed on his feet.

Perspective crept back in. Ollie braced himself for the reality of standing bare-chested in front of Shay to kick him in the nuts. But it didn't happen. Shay was tired, both from touring and the blood-sugar crisis that still wasn't over. However Ollie felt about the events of the last ten minutes, Shay needed to rest.

Shay needed *him*.

"Come on." He kissed Shay one more time, then reluctantly detached himself from Shay's grip. "Get into bed. I'll go get your stuff."

Shay nodded and sat down abruptly, as though the wind had been knocked out of him. He winced, but waved Ollie away. "I'm fine."

Ollie hurried to the living room to fetch Shay's bag. Back in the bedroom, a quick finger prick revealed that Shay's blood sugar was still too low.

"It'll be like this for a while," Shay said in a tone that would've been cross if he hadn't been so tired. "Up and down, adjustments every ten fucking minutes. It sucks, but it's not always this bad, in case you're wondering if I'm a permanent basket case."

"I wasn't." Ollie handed Shay a plate of cheese on toast. "The only reason I'd be relieved that it's not always like this is for your sake."

Shay sighed. "It's the tour, I think. At home, I can have days when I forget I even have diabetes, I mean apart from the tests. I can go weeks sometimes without a low, and I never get highs unless I'm super stressed and run down."

"Are you super stressed?"

"Not anymore."

Ollie made an executive decision not to pull at that thread. It was five o'clock in the morning and he was done with the heavy. He brought his knees to his chest and wrapped his arms around them. He'd put the heating on, but the air still held a chill. Putting his T-shirt back on was the obvious answer, but after so long fighting to keep himself hidden, something inside him wouldn't let him do it. He didn't feel set free, but he felt... something.

It helped that Shay hadn't mentioned it. That he seemed able to casually touch Ollie's skin without truly looking at it. *I can do this.*

Shay finished eating. Ollie took the plate and passed him his medical bag. When he got back from the kitchen, Shay was lying flat on his back, staring at the ceiling, legs half under the covers.

Ollie slid into bed beside him. "You wanna sleep?"

"Yes. No. Maybe."

It was such a complete echo of Ollie's own mind that he laughed. Shay blinked and then laughed too, though his bemusement was clear.

Ollie drew the duvet up and over them, then lay back against the pillows and lifted his good arm. "How about I stick the TV on, eh? We can watch some shit and see what happens."

In answer, Shay wriggled across the bed and slid his long

slender body against Ollie, threw his leg over Ollie's thighs, and dropped his head on Ollie's chest. It was more perfect than terrifying, and Ollie buried a hand in Shay's still-damp hair. He pressed his lips to the crown of Shay's head and rubbed the back of his neck.

Shay was asleep in moments.

CHAPTER TWENTY

WAKING UP in unfamiliar places was Shay's normal, but on the bus, no matter where they ended up, the bed—narrow and short—was always the same.

Ollie's bed was different. Soft and warm, and finally a pillow that smelled like him. A redundant pillow, as it turned out, because Ollie was *right there.*

Ignoring his lingering gut ache, Shay slowly sat up to gaze at his sleeping bedmate. *Wow.* Ollie's handsome looks had always knocked Shay for six, even when he'd tried so hard to hide from Shay, and like this, dead asleep in his own bed, he took Shay's breath away.

Unbidden, Shay's eyes drifted to the mass of scars that covered Ollie's left side. The shock he'd expected to hit him last night—or this morning... whenever Ollie had lost his shit and flung his T-shirt away—was still absent, perhaps because Ollie had spent every moment since he'd revealed to Shay that the scars existed convincing Shay he'd never see them. Or maybe it was another insulin crisis clouding Shay's brain.

Or maybe Shay just wasn't shocked. Maybe the sadness in his heart was enough. Not because Ollie's perfect body was no longer perfect, but because he'd been hurt. Was still hurting. Even though the scars were long healed.

Shay's fingers itched to touch Ollie. To trace the raised flesh and commit it to memory before Ollie pushed him away again. But Shay didn't touch Ollie. He tore his gaze away from the scars and instead lost himself in Ollie's strong chest and subtly ripped abs. Because Ollie's body *was* perfect. More than that. Ollie was beautiful, and that he didn't know it broke Shay's heart.

Ollie shifted in his sleep. He rolled over, reaching for something. Shay offered his hand. Ollie took it and stilled, his face as peaceful as Shay had ever seen it.

Careful not to jostle him, Shay plucked his medical bag from the bedside table and managed a one-handed blood test, a skill he'd perfected years ago when he'd refused to put his harmonica down long enough to use both hands. His levels had tipped high again. He shot some insulin, then lay back down. He'd need to eat soon, but right now, there was nothing on earth that would make him leave this bed. *Just five more minutes.*

"Hmm? Wha—" Shay opened his eyes. Somehow he'd dozed off again and wound up with his head dumped on Ollie's abdomen. *Shit.* "Sorry."

He started to sit up.

Ollie eased him back down. "It's okay. I was wondering if you needed anything. You told me not to let you sleep all day."

"Did I?"

"Yeah. You don't remember?"

Shay let out an unintelligible sound. "I feel like I've had twenty pints every night for the last year."

"That bad?"

Shay sighed and forced himself to sit up enough to meet Ollie's gaze. "It's not that bad, actually. I'll have to nudge my insulin levels for a little while longer, but I'm over it. I can feel it."

"Good."

"It's not good if it means you're kicking me out of your bed."

"You'd rather be ill?"

Shay stuck his tongue out, hoping Ollie had heard what he hadn't said. "What time is it?"

"Two o'clock."

"In the morning?"

"Nah. It's afternoon, mate."

Ollie could've told Shay anything, and he'd have believed him. And with zero clue of how much time had passed since his one-handed blood test, Shay repeated the process, and for the first time in what felt like a week, his levels were within a range he didn't need to worry about.

"I'll make some breakfast in a bit," Ollie said.

"You have food in your house? Wow. I'm impressed. When I go home after a tour it's to the bread I forgot to throw out and some rancid milk."

"I have a housekeeper. She knew I was probably coming back this week, so she left some stuff in the fridge. I have a pretty well-stocked freezer too. I was brought up on batch cooking."

"That sounds amazing. I ate boiled ham and potatoes every Sunday for my entire childhood."

"Nothing wrong with that."

"Oh, I know. But once I discovered curry, I was a goner."

"Well, I don't have any curry stashed away, but I've probably got something spicy enough to make up for it."

On cue, Shay stomach rumbled.

Ollie laughed. "Okay. I'm going to grab a shower, then make some breakfast. You want coffee?"

"No, thank you. Is it okay if I get up and nose around your flat?"

"Of course."

Ollie rolled out of bed with a grace it was impossible to have on a cramped bus. There was a T-shirt on a nearby chair. He hesitated. Shay wanted to tell him it was okay to reach for it and cover up, but Ollie left the room before he could speak—without the T-shirt.

His back was less scarred than his front. As he got further

away, Shay couldn't see them at all. And then he was gone, and the shower turned on, and Shay suddenly felt alone.

I miss him.

How the fuck did we even get here?

No answers were forthcoming from his subconscious, so he got up and ventured out of the bedroom. Ollie's flat was half the size of the house Shay owned in Derby but somehow seemed to have more character. He had artwork on the walls, bookshelves heaving with books, and photographs too. Lots of photographs.

Shay peered at one of a much younger Ollie, all skinny and short-haired, fresh out of school, and then another when he'd clearly been a student. Uni life had suited him, if the wide grin Shay didn't recognise was anything to go by.

"I thought I was happy then."

Shay jumped and threw a glance over his shoulder. "You weren't happy?"

"Not really. I was in a toxic relationship with a bloke who broke my heart. And got me hooked on ciggies, the bastard." Ollie came up behind Shay and picked up a different photo frame. "I was happy in this one—it was just after I got my first BBC contract."

"Before the accident?"

"Uh-huh." Ollie set the photo frame down. "I'd given up the binge drinking and sex parties by then. Shamefully, I was in danger of growing up."

"Sex parties?"

Ollie's faint grin turned sardonic. "I'm joking. Mostly. I was a horrible twenty-something."

"How old are you now? Fuck, I can't believe I don't know."

"I'm thirty-one."

"I thought you were older... then I thought you were younger. You have one of those faces it's hard to tell."

"I'm gonna take that as a compliment and move on."

"You should."

Ollie snorted. "Whatever. You're a nosy fuck, so do you want to see my parents?"

Of course Shay did. Ollie knew him far too well.

Ollie's parents looked exactly as Shay had pictured them. Dark-haired, dark-eyed, and gorgeous.

"Your dad is so handsome."

"Thanks, I think. Don't tell him that, though. He's a big enough tart as it is."

Shay laughed. "What about your mum? What's she like?"

"Complicated. I don't speak to her much, but we're close, if that makes sense?"

"It does; Ben's like that with his folks. Only sees them at Christmas, and it's like they've never been apart."

Ollie hummed softly. "I should see them more—my grandparents too—but I got hooked on my own miserable company, and it's a tough habit to quit."

"Not impossible, though." Shay turned around to face Ollie. Found him shirtless still and damp from the shower. His hands twitched again, and this time he couldn't keep them to himself.

He laid his hand over Ollie's heart, his palm covering smooth skin and his fingertips grazing the web of scars snaking down from Ollie's shoulder. Blood thundered in Shay's ears, but he couldn't tell if it was his own pulse jumping or Ollie's.

His other hand found its way to Ollie's right hip, left bare by Ollie's low-slung sweatpants. There was no scarring there, and Shay couldn't help drawing Ollie closer and sliding his hand up Ollie's back. "Does it still hurt?"

"My skin?"

"Yeah."

"No. It was a mess for a long time, but what you see is what you get now."

"It's healed?"

"I guess. I've called it other words in the past."

Shay didn't want to know how else Ollie would describe it. He let his hand slip from Ollie's chest and down his torso to his ribcage, where the scars were thickest.

Ollie flinched, and then he shivered, but he didn't pull away.

Emboldened, Shay ghosted his fingertips up and down, not

pressing too hard, but firm enough that it was real… for both of them. The scars were nothing like he'd ever felt before, but then, touching Ollie had always been like this. Heat crept through Shay as he tentatively explored every part of Ollie he could reach, breath caught as he braced himself for Ollie to stop him.

But Ollie didn't stop him. He watched, apparently fascinated, as Shay's hand roamed his body, and said nothing at all.

"Can you feel it?" Shay whispered.

"I feel *you*," Ollie said. "And I feel weird, like I'm looking down on myself from somewhere else—fuck."

Shay's thumb brushed Ollie's nipple. Ollie made a sound low in his throat. Shay's blood rushed impossibly faster, and more heat pooled in his groin. *I have to kiss him.*

Their lips met, like they had so many times before, but it was different now. Barriers Shay had never even seen faded away, and suddenly he was back on his bus bunk, fist shoved in his mouth as Ollie blew him into oblivion.

Ollie had been wearing jeans that night, any obvious signs of arousal masked by denim, but the sweatpants he wore now did little to conceal the effect Shay's kiss was having on him. Another jolt passed through Shay. He hooked a leg over Ollie's hip and kissed him harder, and then he was moving as Ollie backed him into the hallway.

"Bedroom," Ollie gasped out between kisses. "I don't want to wind up on the floor."

That they were going to wind up anywhere left Shay dizzy. He broke the kiss and grabbed Ollie's hand, towing him swiftly into the bedroom and kicking the door shut for no reason whatsoever.

He pushed Ollie onto the bed and straddled him, reclaiming his lips. He was careful of Ollie's scars at first, keeping his full weight off him, but Ollie growled and yanked him down, and there wasn't an inch between them.

Clothes disappeared. Shay didn't know how, just that he was naked, and Ollie was too, and it was wonderful and magical and nowhere near enough. *I need more.*

They were already slick. Shay ground against Ollie over and

over, sending shockwaves of pleasure through them both. Their kisses grew from sweet to rough—demanding—and a sharp coil burned in Shay's gut. "I want—" He stopped. *Don't say that.* "I—"

Ollie covered Shay's mouth with his hand. "Do it. I want you to."

It was everything Shay needed to hear.

Ollie scooted back on the bed and jerked his head at the bedside table.

Shay followed his direction and retrieved everything they needed from the drawer. He rolled a condom on and crawled between Ollie's legs. Lifted them. Bent them. Made a cradle for himself so perfect he almost fucking cried.

He hunched over Ollie and kissed him for the thousandth time, his tongue gently demanding entrance as he coaxed Ollie open with his fingers, swallowing Ollie's hitched moan.

Ollie was tight and wet and hot. So fucking hot. Shay withdrew his fingers and eased inside him with a long, torturous slide. Ollie enveloped him, and a wave of sensation so intense it shook his entire body rocked through him.

Shay groaned. "Oh fuck."

But beneath him, Ollie trembled, his eyes screwed shut, body tense. It wasn't there for him yet, it was hurting.

Shay moved in gentle circles, chasing the magical cadence that would free Ollie from the stretching burn. Slowly, the painful tension disappeared and bliss spread across Ollie's beautiful face. He wrapped his legs around Shay, arching his body to take him deeper, and threw his head back.

"Fuck yeah."

His gravelly curse spurred Shay on. He fucked him harder and faster, the drumbeat of ecstasy banging in time with the headboard against the wall.

Ollie was trapped between them, his hard length pressed against Shay's abdomen. Shay closed a hand around him and squeezed. Everything got hotter, and blunt nails dug into Shay's back. He moaned and fought the hurricane rushing up on him. "Ollie—"

"Do it." Ollie caught him in his fierce gaze. "I'm gonna come so hard."

Shay was gone. He tumbled over the edge so fast he never saw it coming. Release hit him like a truck. He cried out, and the careful pace he'd set turned frantic, chasing the amazing sounds Ollie gasped out as he followed Shay off the cliff.

Wet warmth pulsed between them. Shay opened his eyes, and it was over. His shoulders heaved and his chest burned. *Did that really just happen?*

"Shay." Ollie's grip was still vice-like on Shay's chin. "Look at me."

Disoriented, Shay focused on Ollie. Fuck, he'd dreamed of seeing him like this, blissed out and smiling, chest flushed with pleasure. So many long nights and long days when all he knew of Ollie was his tight shoulders and set jaw. His chain-smoking and dead stare. He wondered if Ollie knew how alive he looked right now.

Shay gently withdrew and left the bed to bin the condom. When he came back, Ollie had barely moved.

"I need another shower."

"Me too." Shay curled around him, fatigue fast replacing the sated glow in his soul. "Can we lie here for a bit first, though?"

"Mate, I ain't going anywhere."

"Promise?"

"I promise, Shay."

CHAPTER TWENTY-ONE

OLLIE DIDN'T go back to sleep. Instead he watched over Shay and read the news on his phone, all the while trying not to freak the fuck out over the insanity of the last twelve hours. *You let him fuck you.* More than that, he'd let Shay love him, and now his body was on fire with the best kind of heat. His scars tingled where Shay had touched him, and he realised with a start that he wanted Shay to touch him again, and to keep on touching him until Shay begged to let him stop.

He was upside down. He was sure of it. Shay had always made him feel like someone brand new that even Ollie didn't recognise, but he was sorely unprepared for the barrage of contentment his heart sent out to combat the doubts in his brain. He searched for regret but found nothing but love.

Love. Fucking-A. Could he do that? Could he love Shay? Because his heart already knew that Shay loved him. It was in every gentle touch and kind word. Every fierce glare when Ollie was being a dick. And Shay deserved to be loved so hard in return. Cherished. Adored. Could Ollie be that man?

A year ago, hell, even a week ago, Ollie would've said no. Now he wanted to be that man so badly his chest ached. The need to take care of Shay was overwhelming, and it was only the necessity of food that drove him from the bed.

The Tupperware pot he'd retrieved from the freezer last night was still in the sink. He chucked its contents in a pan to heat up, dug out some *kopytka* to go with it, and put a pan of water on the stove to boil. The tiny potato dumplings took minutes to cook, and by then, his grandmother's goulash was heated through.

He was digging around for matching bowls when Shay shuffled into the kitchen, sleepy gaze halfway between alarmed and confused until it fell on Ollie.

"There you are."

He thought I left. Pain lanced Ollie's heart. Crockery forgotten, he straightened and closed the stride-length distance between them. He pulled Shay into the kind of embrace that lasted forever, and Shay sagged against him, his obvious relief cutting Ollie to the bone.

He nosed Shay's hair out of his face. "Are you ready to eat?"

"Uh-huh." After a long pause, Shay raised his head. "That's what woke me up. It smells like that place you sent me to up north."

"Good. Then I made it right. You liked the goulash, didn't you?"

"Loved it." Shay peered around Ollie, and his expression brightened. "I've been dreaming about it ever since. Did you seriously make this?"

"I did. Can't remember when, though. It's been in the freezer a while."

"You're so organised."

"First time for everything, eh? Seriously, though, it's a Polish thing. In my family, the men cook as much as the women. More, probably. We like it."

"You'll have to teach me."

Warmth replaced pain. "I'd like that."

Ollie sent Shay to the couch and followed him with their dinner… lunch—whatever it was. "You want a beer?"

Shay shook his head. "Fuck that noise. I need a detox."

Ollie couldn't argue with that. It was only driving the van that saved his liver from coming home pickled.

They ate in companionable silence, the glow of what they'd left in the bedroom still burning bright between them. Emotions Ollie couldn't name rippled through him, and it didn't seem to matter how close he sat to Shay, it wasn't close enough.

Shay disappeared to check his sugar level. When he came back, he looked better than he had in days. "I think it's over."

Relief washed over Ollie. He'd blocked out how much seeing Shay so incapacitated had scared him, but with the shadow gone —for now—everything seemed lighter. He held out his hand. Shay took it and dropped back onto the couch beside him.

"We have thirty-six hours," he said. "What do you want to do?"

Ollie could think of plenty of things, all of them involving little or no clothes, and more self-imposed restraint slipped away. "You know, before the, uh, accident, I was a bit of a slag—different fella every night—but after, I never slept with anyone until you."

If Shay was taken aback by Ollie's extreme answer to his benign question, it didn't show. He lolled his head on Ollie's shoulder. "I've slept with, like, four people my entire life, and two of them were girls. I mean, I love sex, but I have a hard time separating it from my emotions, so I've only ever done it with people I lo—um, have strong feelings for."

Ollie caught the slip. It ricocheted in every fibre of himself. *I love you too.* He rested his cheek on Shay's head. "Larry told me your last boyfriend was a bit of a dick."

Shay snorted. "He was. It was my fault, though."

"How so?"

"I let him get away with being a manipulative wanker, so he kept doing it."

"That doesn't make it your fault."

Shay made a noncommittal noise. "It doesn't make me blameless either."

Ollie wanted to punch whoever had made Shay believe that he was worth anything less than the whole damn world. Then he recalled every moment he'd left Shay hanging, run from him, leaving nothing but bewilderment and hurt feelings in his wake, and realised he was no better than anyone who'd come before. "I'm so fucking sorry."

Shay shifted so he could stare at Ollie. "What for?"

"For being so weird about stuff. I wish I'd told you from the start about... everything."

"Why? So we could bang on the bus and do this with an audience?" Shay gestured around the living room. "I can't even begin to understand what you've been through, so cut yourself some slack, okay? We're here now."

We're here now. Shay etched another indelible mark on Ollie's heart, but it wasn't enough. Ollie shook his head. "You don't need to understand. I just... I need to get over it, and I know that."

Shay slid off the couch so fast he blurred. He dropped to his knees and forced himself between Ollie's legs. "Get over it? Why? Something horrific happened to you."

"Did it?"

"I don't—what?" Shay shook his head too, as if to clear it. "What are you trying to say?"

Ollie took a deep breath and tried to verbalise the jumble in his head. "I didn't feel it... when it happened. I watched my arm burn, but I didn't feel it. It didn't hurt, and it was weeks before the pain kicked in. For the longest time, I thought it was a bad dream."

"But it wasn't a dream. Adrenaline from the crash and other injuries could've stopped you feeling it at the time, and then you'd have been dosed up on painkillers in hospital—fuck, I don't know, but don't tell me it didn't hurt, Ollie, because I don't believe you."

"It did hurt," Ollie said. "Only not when I expected it to, and I felt bad about that. It haunted me, so it started happening in my sleep instead."

"Actual bad dreams?"

"Sometimes... or it would be a replay. It's not a dream if it's real, right?"

"No, it's a flashback, and probably classed as PTSD."

A sneer threatened. Ollie beat it back and shook his head. "They tested me for that. I didn't have it."

"When?"

"What?"

"When did they test you for PTSD?"

"In hospital, after I left the burn unit."

"Not since?"

"No." Ollie couldn't quite work out how they'd got to this point. How they'd gone from eating his grandmother's goulash to Shay clearly thinking he was out of his damn mind. And he didn't know how to get back to the place where Shay smiled at him instead of the concerned frown he wore now. "Look," he said quietly. "I know I'm fucked up, but you should've seen me a year ago. There's no way I'd have been able to ride your tour bus all over the country."

"What changed?"

Ollie shrugged. "Nothing. Everything. I got bored with wallowing in my own misery, and so I started forcing myself to do things that scared me."

Shay squeezed Ollie's knees. "Like being a passenger on the road?"

"Yeah. I still hate it—it's like I'm waiting for the engine to cut out and blow up all the time—but it's not as shit as it used to be."

"Do you think maybe...?" Shay bit his lip. "Do you think if you had some help it could ever not be shit at all? I mean, I know it'd never go away, but you shouldn't have to suffer, Ollie. What happened to you wasn't your fault."

"What you live with isn't your fault either."

"I was born with it, and I'm not traumatised by being diabetic. It's not the same thing at all, and you know it."

Ollie did know it, but the suffocating cloud that came with talking about things he never talked about was starting to overwhelm him. Shay's touch tied him down to the world, but he needed more. "I woke up after the accident with this grindstone churning in my head, telling me everything was broken. Some days I still feel it grinding."

"But not every day?"

"Not so much when you're around."

Shay's smile was sad. Ollie pried Shay's hands from his knees and twined their fingers together, tugging until Shay straightened enough for Ollie to kiss him. Shay gasped. The spark between them ignited, and this was a fire Ollie wasn't afraid of. He'd put a T-shirt on while he'd cooked. Shay took it off and tossed it away.

The kiss deepened, only for Shay to pull back. He stood and vanished. Panic seized Ollie, but Shay was back before he could blink, brandishing all he needed to make Ollie forget everything except how to feel.

And how to fly.

CHAPTER TWENTY-TWO

WHEN IT was over, they lay panting and naked on the couch. Ollie trembled. Shay hadn't been as cautious with him this time, and Ollie hadn't let him try, as though he'd craved pain and pleasure to free him from something else.

Shay understood that. Losing himself in Ollie was magic, and as release had pulsed through him and into Ollie, he'd almost forgotten the conversation that had brought them there.

Almost, because he'd never forget Ollie's haunted gaze.

He pressed his palm over Ollie's thumping heart. Ollie opened his eyes. He smiled, and Shay smiled too. "You're back."

Ollie chuckled drowsily. "That's the second time you've fucked me into a coma."

"To be fair, I did it to myself the first time too."

"Uh-huh." Ollie shifted onto his side, wincing. "For what it's worth, I'm glad this didn't happen on the bus."

"Me too." Shay kissed Ollie's cheek, then got up, padding nude across the room to the bag he'd abandoned when he'd first arrived at the flat. Inside were his harmonica, penny whistle, and the instrument Ollie had gifted him.

He brought the unnamed instrument back to the couch. "You still won't tell me what it's called?"

"Nope. I'd like to see you play it, though."

Shay snorted and turned the instrument over in his hands. It was the size of a ukulele and had strings, but it also had a wind-up handle, accordion-like keys, decks, and tuning pegs. It was a melting pot of the familiar and the downright bizarre, and he didn't have the first clue where to start. "I'll play it if you play me some guitar."

Ollie rolled his eyes. "I'm not playing the guitar for you—I'm shite. Give me that thing, though. I might still be able to crank something out of it."

Shay relinquished the mutant accordion and watched, fascinated, as Ollie ran his hands over it, apparently more at home with it than he wanted Shay to know.

"This is a small one," Ollie said. "Traditionally, they can be huge. Some even take two people to play."

"If you want me to play with you, sweetheart, you've just gotta ask."

"Very funny."

"I try."

"Try harder."

"Harder. Right there." Shay shivered as his mind took him back, unbidden, to their lovemaking on the couch minutes ago. He fought hard to focus on how Ollie was handling the strange instrument, but it was... hard. *Dammit.* "Um, so how do you play it?"

"Like this."

Ollie turned the handle at the base of the instrument. A plaintive sound rose up from it, settling into an ethereal bass note. He pressed a few keys, and a simple melody played out, but with the bass notes coming from the turning handle, the finished sound was so complex Shay's breath caught.

"Wow," he whispered. "Keep going."

Ollie chuckled. "I'll have to go in a loop, this is the only tune I know."

"I don't care. Keep going."

Ollie kept going, and the sound of the instrument filled the living room—delicate, and yet uncompromising. Drifting, and yet so entirely in Shay's consciousness that he leaned closer and closer to Ollie until their heads bumped.

Finally, Ollie stopped. "You want a go?"

Shay all but snatched the instrument from him. "What were you playing?"

"You didn't recognise it?"

"No. Was it a traditional song from wherever I come from that you won't tell me?"

"It was 'Lucy in the Sky with Diamonds.' That's pretty much all I can play on the guitar too."

Shay experimentally turned the handle, nerves stretched to breaking until a sound he recognised as Ollie's came out. Ollie said more words, but Shay didn't hear him. Barely noticed when Ollie laughed and rose from the couch, kissing the top of Shay's head before he left the room.

Closing his eyes, Shay retraced where Ollie's fingers had been, pressing the keys. The weird Beatles interpretation played out. Shay chased it, finding the rest of the melody with the keys, but he lost the bass line. *Fuck.*

He went back to the start. *This is gonna take a while.*

"I DON'T want to go out." Shay stood mutinously in the shower while Ollie washed his hair. "I want to stay in and finish that song."

"I know that, but you're going back to work tomorrow, and you need some vitamin D."

"It's getting dark."

"Okay. You need some fresh air, then."

"We're in London."

"Do as you're fucking told."

Ollie spoke with a grin that warmed Shay's heart, but he was distracted. He'd been obsessively playing the instrument Ollie had given him for endless hours, but the technicalities of the bass line still eluded him. With internet research banned, he was feeling his way in the dark, and only Ollie himself had ever caused Shay so much frustration.

It didn't help that Ollie seemed to find it hilarious.

It always helped to see Ollie laugh.

Shay glowered at him anyway. "Where do you even want to go? You have the world's best food in your freezer."

"Not the world's best," Ollie corrected. "It's an interpretation, and if you'll stop moaning and put some clothes on, I'll prove it to you."

"Fine."

Shay grumbled all the way through getting dressed and leaving the house but shut up sharply when Ollie led him to a bus stop. *Perspective, mate. Perspective.*

They stood close together on the crowded bus, close enough that Shay could slide his hand under Ollie's clothes and stroke his bare hip, but not so close that he could tell if Ollie's heart was slamming anxiously against his ribcage. If it wasn't for Ollie's teeth worrying his bottom lip, and his white knuckles, Shay wouldn't have known he was struggling at all.

The bus took them to Waltham Forest. Shay searched his "Ollie" memories and recalled it was the borough where Ollie had grown up.

They got off the bus by the Tube station. Shay jerked his head at it. "It wouldn't have been quicker to take the Underground?"

"It would," Ollie said. "But I make myself take the bus when I'm feeling brave. Besides, you don't see anything on the Tube."

Fair enough. Shay glanced around at the bustling street. Like most working class areas in London, it was a heady mix of vibrance and grime. It was wonderful—and terrifying.

Ollie led him across the road and down a few streets, pointing things out along the way. "The Olympic Park is over there, the 491 Gallery is round the corner to the left. If you like drill music we could swing through Walthamstow."

"That's not the same as Waltham Forest?"

"Not quite." Ollie spun on his heels again and pointed in a different direction. "Over there is where the German airships dropped bombs in the First World War. I'll take you there in daylight one day."

"Why?"

"Because it means something."

"To me?"

"To everyone."

As ever, Ollie's cryptic answers meant everything and nothing. Shay wanted to punch him, to kiss him, but on the busy London street, he simply trailed Ollie to a block of sheltered housing flats around the corner from the market.

"Where are we?"

Ollie fished a set of keys from his pocket. "My grandparents' house."

Despite where they were, he'd have surprised Shay more if he'd said the moon, but there was no time to react. Only connect.

Ollie led him to a ground-floor flat and opened the door. Immediately the scent of paprika from the Newcastle cafe hit Shay, and he felt at home. Voices reached them. An elderly woman with a headscarf appeared in the hallway and then a man with a cane. They had dark eyes and kind smiles. They were *Ollie*, and so obviously pleased to see him that Shay almost cried.

Again. *Fuck my life.*

SHAY PUSHED his bowl away. He could've eaten gallons of the *amazing* cabbage and sausage broth Ollie's grandmother—Oliwia—had served him, but his blood sugar wouldn't thank him for overeating. He caught Ollie's eye.

Ollie nodded, and Shay excused himself to the bathroom.

When he came back, Ollie had disappeared with his grandfather, leaving Shay with Oliwia in the kitchen.

She brought a cake covered in poppy seeds to the table and cut Shay a slice small enough that it wouldn't kill him. "No sugar.

Just lemon and honey. We don't eat many cakes around here, so they must be good."

Her accent was Ollie's, but her delivery was rougher. And somehow she knew Shay couldn't handle a sugar-laden treat right now. "Thank you."

"It is okay. Ollie told me you're a good boy."

"When did he tell you that?"

"A while ago. He doesn't call us often. We are happy to see him now."

A while ago. Shay wondered what that meant. He'd known Ollie barely a month, and their relationship had been… complicated from the start. "I think he's happy to see you too. He misses your cooking."

Oliwia made a clicking sound with her teeth. "Of course he does. When you are Polish, only the food of your homeland will make you right. I told him all the time when he was at school and eating all that McDonalds rubbish."

"He didn't get much Polish food on the road with the band. I did, though. He sent me to, uh, Eryk's cafe in Newcastle."

Oliwia scowled. "Eryk is from his father's side. His goulash is wrong."

"It's different to yours?"

"Of course. Mine is authentic."

The only difference Shay could recall between the goulash he'd eaten in Newcastle and the one from Ollie's freezer was the slightly thicker consistency of Eryk's, but he held his tongue. How many times had he heard his own relatives bicker about the best way to mash a potato?

Oliwia brought coffee to the table too. It was thick and dark, like the brutal potion Ollie drank every morning. Shay yearned for a bucket of sugar to ease the bitterness but powered through, distracting himself by glancing around the colourful kitchen. It was untidy in the best way—strings of sausages hanging from the ceiling and a sack of caraway seeds in the corner. A jet-black cat wandered in and jumped up on the counter. No one shooed it down.

I like it here. Shay settled back in his seat. After a while, he stopped missing Ollie.

"You should go and see your mother," Feodor said.

Ollie glanced up from the Sky box he was trying to mend so his grandfather could binge watch *On the Buses*. "I will. Maybe. I'm hitting the road again tomorrow, so it might have to wait until I get back."

"Why do you keep your mother waiting so much?"

"Because she's as busy as I am. Every time I go round, there's no one there."

"So pick up the phone first. Not everyone can be old and housebound like us."

"You're not housebound. I bet you were down the bingo hall last night."

Feodor's sheepish grin said it all, but his searching stare remained. Ollie sighed and took another screw out of the Sky box. His grandparents had always been like this: Feodor would take him apart with his quiet interrogations while Oliwia would kill him with kindness and food. It was worse than his parents' nagging, but he never managed to stay away for long.

"Your friend is nice," Feodor said. "Where's he from?"

"Derby."

"I meant where is his family from?"

"I know you did, but I can't tell you that because I haven't told him. I'm making a documentary about Shay's family tree, remember?"

"Oh yes." Feodor's cloudy gaze briefly cleared. "And now you have fallen in love with your subject. That's a TV show in itself, no?"

Ollie needed a cigarette. Thankfully, Feodor puffed liked a chimney, so lighting up indoors wasn't an issue. He chain-smoked three while he finished up with the Sky box and skirted round Feodor's obvious curiosity about Shay.

Oliwia brought coffee and cake, but Ollie waved it away. "Thanks, but we should get going. Shay's going back to work tomorrow."

"I know," Oliwia said. "He told me, and he likes my cake. You can bring him again."

Shay appeared behind her, looking more awake than Ollie had expected to see him. "It's true, but we should probably go. I have some things to finish up before tomorrow."

By things, he almost certainly meant the composition he was picking his way through on the instrument Ollie had given him. Watching Shay master it with little more than instinct had been enchanting, but Ollie was fairly sure his neighbours didn't agree. Still. Ollie didn't know his neighbours, and he owned the freehold on his flat, so who the fuck cared?

They said goodbye. Oliwia hugged Shay hard, and Feodor didn't remind Ollie again to go and see his mother. But he didn't have to. Feodor said a lot, but often the message was in what he chose not to say.

At the Underground station, Shay bounced down the escalators, brimming with energy. "I like your grandparents."

"So do I." Ollie eyed Shay's twitching hands and darting gaze. "Jesus, how much coffee did you drink?"

"Two mugs. Black. No sugar. I think I'm going to be awake for a week."

Ollie didn't argue. He was used to nuclear Polish coffee. Shay was used to PG Tips.

On the platform, Shay wandered up and down with the fascination of someone who didn't live in London. Ollie leaned against the grubby wall and watched him, transfixed as ever but his mind also elsewhere. Kind of. The last few days with Shay had been a bubble of emotion. He was exhausted by it, but not ready to let it go. The sense of being on the edge of the rest of his life was all-consuming, but Ollie didn't know how to jump. He had to work harder on himself, he knew that. But how?

A train pulled into the station. The pushback blew Shay's hair out of his face. With his caffeine-widened eyes, he seemed wild, and Ollie craved that freedom more than anything.

They got on the train. Ollie pushed Shay into the corner of a carriage and took his hands. "When you go back to the tour tomorrow, I'm not coming with you."

CHAPTER TWENTY-THREE

Ollie left the van in a car park behind the O2 Academy in Brixton. Fred and Khalid were bringing a friend back with them to help with the roadie work while Ollie was gone, and they had a spare key. There was no reason for Ollie to hang around, but he found himself drifting towards the bus anyway.

It was empty, obviously, like the van. The band were in rehearsals, and he and Shay had said their goodbyes hours ago. But still. The bus seemed like the right place to be, even though he knew it wasn't.

He sat on Shay's bed and tore a page out of a notebook. He stole a pencil from Shay's stash and scrawled the words he'd already said out loud.

I am coming back

Then he tucked the note under Shay's pillow and left the bus.

Heart heavy, he took the Underground back to his flat. He had a lot to do before he could think about sharing a bed with Shay again, but first, he had a mountain of work to catch up on. Driving the van, running the roadie crew, and spending every other free moment either with Shay or thinking about him, had set him way behind.

At home, he set up his equipment in the small alcove he used as an office. He sat down and shivered. Even through his clothes, after weeks on the road, the leather chair felt strange against his skin, scarred and smooth. *Everything* felt strange.

I'm not the same person.

The thought was errant at first, but as Shay's face filled the huge monitor Ollie used at home, he knew it was true. He clicked through frame after frame of footage, cataloguing Shay's every emotion as Ollie had revealed his colourful history. Curiosity became fascination. Sadness became grief. And then a rare frame where the camera had caught them both—staring at each other, naturally. Shay's gaze was fire. Ollie's was guarded, but Ollie knew if he continued to scroll through the footage, that would change.

I'm not the same person.

The echo was louder this time and brought with it a creeping feeling that drove Ollie out of his chair. Shay was everything Ollie had never known he wanted, but Ollie wasn't enough for him, not like this. He'd walked away from Shay with a plan—a plan that would be on hold until he'd caught up with his work—but Ollie was done waiting.

I need to start living.

He backed out of the office and into the kitchen. His phone was on the counter. He opened the family WhatsApp group he rarely participated in and tapped out a text.

Ollie: *Mum, I need help.*

They sat in the living room. Ollie's childhood home was a riot of colour, but a lifetime had passed since he had last noticed. His parents, Jannah and Wit, were on either side of him, not touching him—they'd learned not to since the accident—but close enough so he sensed them, even with his eyes closed.

His eyes weren't closed, though, metaphorically or otherwise. For the first time in years, he was entirely present. "I met someone."

Wit blinked, surprised. But Jannah nodded. Of the two of them, Ollie's mother was the most intuitive. "A boy?"

"A man, actually, but yeah."

"So it is more than a friendship?"

"I'm trying for it to be."

Wit got up and walked to the fireplace. His reflection in the large mirror gave him nowhere to hide, and as he ran a large hand through his dark hair, Ollie saw the cogs in his brain turning, searching for the correlation between this revelation and Ollie's plea for help. Ollie's parents were practical people. "Where did you meet him?"

"At work. He's in the band I'm on tour with."

"A musician?"

"Yeah."

"That's nice," Jannah said. "Can we meet him?"

"Not yet. I mean, I want you to, but that's kind of why I'm here. I-I need to fix some shit before... fuck, this is coming out wrong." Ollie took a deep breath. "Mum, I'm so messed-up. You know I am, and I can't put all that on him. It's not fair."

"What are you asking us for, son?" Wit turned away from the mirror. "You want us to take you to the place at Gubałówka?"

"No, Dad. I don't want to go up a mountain to find myself, I'm right here. I just... I need... I don't know what I need, okay? But I know I can't do it on my own."

It was the frankest conversation Ollie could ever remember having with his parents. Jannah got up and left the room. Wit took her place. "We always wanted to help."

"I know."

"So what's changed? You can't want to get better for someone else, son. It has to be for you."

"It is for me."

"Are you sure?"

"Yes, Dad. I'm sure."

Jannah came back. In her hand, she clutched a thick brown envelope. "Trauma counsellors," she said. "We knew it couldn't be just anybody, so we searched and searched for you, hoping one day you would let us help you."

Ollie took the envelope. His hands shook, but he let them. Let his parents see it, absorb it, and know they'd done the right thing. "Are they in London? I meant it when I said I didn't want to go to bloody Poland."

Jannah rolled her eyes. "So difficult without even trying. Yes, in London, most of them. Do you want to look?"

"Yeah. I think I do."

CHAPTER TWENTY-FOUR

I AM coming back

For the thousandth time, Shay unfolded the note, read it, and refolded it into the tiny square Ollie had left it in. Four words. They meant everything, but in moments like these, alone in his bunk, Shay wondered if they meant anything at all.

It had been three long days since Ollie had left the tour—and Shay—behind. Three long nights. Ollie hadn't called, and Shay hadn't either. A million times he'd picked up his phone, only to put it down again when an instinct he didn't quite understand told him to let Ollie be.

Didn't make it easy, though. Sometimes Shay lay awake and remembered the stolen nights in Ollie's flat, when Ollie had been so open and free. Shay's body cried out for Ollie. Ached for him. Then he'd recall the darker moments and realise they outnumbered the occasions he'd seen Ollie truly smile, and his heart hurt.

"Oi, oi, mate." Jumbo dropped, uninvited, into Shay's personal space. "Last London show tonight, then we're back to the north country. Excited?"

"About leaving London?"

"Nah, about going home."

Shay sighed. "We're not going home. We're going to Leeds."

"Yeah, but that's our penultimate stop. What's up? Missing Ollie?"

Shay flinched. No one had mentioned Ollie since Shay had returned from the tour break alone, but if anyone was going to break the unspoken agreement, it was always going to be Jumbo. "Yeah, actually, I am missing him. I got used to having his grumpy arse around."

"Me too, though I'm guessing you have different appreciation for his arse."

"Nice."

Jumbo grinned. "I thought so. Where's he at, anyway? I thought he was filming you for the whole tour."

"He needed some time off."

"Why? The dude's a workaholic."

"That's not reason enough?"

Jumbo reached into his back pocket. He came up with a packet of wine gums and leaned over Shay to do who-the-hell-knew what.

"For your emergency kit," he said when he straightened. "I've been mad googling hypoglycaemia."

"Why?"

"So I know what to do next time."

"It was *hyper*glycaemia last time, mate. But thanks. You're cute."

"I try. Seriously, though, man. Are you worried Ollie ain't gonna come back, cause I'm fairly sure there's more chance of hell freezing over. I saw how he looked at you when you were sick. If he doesn't love you, I'll eat my shoes."

"You'll eat anything."

"You wound me, Shay. Don't be a dick. You know it's true."

Shay rolled onto his belly and pulled a pillow over his head. It *was* true. He knew Ollie loved him, even though he'd never said it. But when had *Jumbo* become the voice of all reason?

Jumbo grunted and wandered off. Shay listened to him amble down the aisle and exit the bus before he sat up and glanced around. He was alone, and his craving for an Ollie fix was at an all-time high. He picked up his phone. Put it down again. Then reached for his favourite notebook and began to write.

Hey,

So you'll probably never read this, but I need to talk to you, and I don't want to bother you while you're doing… whatever you're doing, so here we are.

I miss you.

I guess that was all I needed to say, but I need you to know it's true. We never got round to saying some of the stuff that matters, and I know we will… when you're ready. But I need you to know I miss you, and I love you. And none of this feels like home without you.

I am who I am, and who I was before I met you, but something shifted when you looked at me that first time. Even if you don't come back, I know nothing will ever be the same. You are coming back, right? Fuck, ignore that. I know you are. And I didn't mean to write a million words telling you all the shit I need.

I just… I want you to know that it's okay. And it will always be okay. I know you're messed-up, and I know you don't want to be.

That's enough, Ollie. It always was.

Shay xx

The word vomit was supposed to be therapeutic, but seeing it on the page felt hollow. Shay fumbled for his phone, snapped a picture of the notebook page, and sent it hurtling through WhatsApp before he could change his mind.

You fool. But it was too late. The image delivered to Ollie's phone. Cringing, Shay buried his phone under his pillow. As though hiding it would somehow take everything back. As though he even wanted to take it back.

He didn't. But he left the phone where it was all the same.

Rehearsal and soundcheck passed in a blur. London crowds were tough, and each gig so far had taken a few tracks to warm up. This show had to go off with a bang, and agonising over the set list kept Shay occupied until frustration boiled over and he tossed the seventh incarnation of it into the bin.

"Whoa, someone's got the hump," Jumbo teased.

No one else said a word, but irritation flooded Shay's veins anyway. He grabbed the nearest instrument—his neglected flute —and left the room. After a moment, footsteps followed him, but he didn't turn round until Mara caught his arm; she hadn't been in the rehearsal room.

"Your phone," she said. "It was ringing, so I brought it back from the bus."

Shay snatched the phone from her, ignoring her knowing wink, and kept walking, not daring to examine the screen until he was alone in the dressing room.

Two missed calls greeted him. His heart sank. Neither was Ollie. One was clearly an arse-dial from Jumbo. Shay sighed and returned the other—his dad.

Frank answered with a grunt. "Thought you'd gone on stage without your good luck charm."

"My good luck charm?"

"Me, of course, lad. You think I don't know you call me every night out of superstition rather than a desperate need to know I've done the dogs and put the dinner on?"

"Git."

"Aye. But it is what it is. You okay? Jumbo told me you had a wobbler a few days ago."

A wobbler. Frank's affectionate term for any blood-sugar glitch that fucked up Shay's day never failed to make Shay smile. "I'm good. It was a hyper... I haven't had one of those for ages."

"Just as well. They knock you for six." Following a pause came the clunk of the ancient cast-iron slow cooker that kept Frank in hot dinners. "Are you eating proper? Getting plenty of rest between gigs and whatnot?"

Shay thought back to the sacred few days he'd spent with Ollie away from the tour—sleeping in his bed, eating his wonderful Polish food, fooling around on his bed, making him—

"Yeah, Dad. I'm looking after myself. Don't worry about that."

Frank grunted again, clearly unconvinced, but he let it go; he always did. Giving Shay grief wasn't his style.

They said their goodbyes. Shay ended the call and stared unseeing at the screen as a sudden wave of homesickness washed over him. Life at his childhood home was as simple as the food, and he yearned for it as much as he did the complexities of being with Ollie.

I want to go home.

But he couldn't. He had a show to play—a big one—and zero idea of how he was going to open it.

Shay dropped his phone on a bench and opened his flute case. He picked the flute up and pieced it together, blowing dust from the lip plate and mechanisms. It seemed like a year since he'd last played it, but in reality, it had only been a few weeks. A month, perhaps. How much could change in that time.

He brought the flute to his lips and sucked in a breath.

His phone rang.

It was Ollie.

SHAY'S HEART jumped at lightning speed, but his arm seemed to move in slow motion as he grabbed the phone, and his tongue felt thick and heavy. "Um, hey."

"What's wrong?"

Shay blinked. Of everything he'd imagined Ollie might say first, it wasn't that. "What makes you think something's wrong?"

"Your voice. You sound like you're choking."

Shay blew out a breath and set his flute on the bench. "I'm okay, I'm just... fuck, I don't know. The show tonight has to be massive—all the record-company execs and media wankers are coming—but I literally have no idea what to play."

In the grand scheme of things, it sounded ridiculous, but as Shay laid a hand over his tight chest, he realised Ollie was right; he was choking.

Ollie hummed thoughtfully. "That wasn't what I expected you to say."

"No?"

"No. But that's probably a good thing. You know what you need to play. You just haven't figured out how to get there."

"That doesn't make any sense."

Ollie chuckled, dark and throaty. "What does? Okay, think about it like this: what makes this gig so important? Apart from the obvious business stuff I know you're not that interested in."

Ollie knew him so well. The band was Shay's life, but as long as he earned a living, the commercial details rarely crossed his mind. If Corina was happy, he was happy. So what was it about this gig that mattered so much?

He sat on the bench and ran a finger over his flute. "I guess it's because we never thought we'd get here. The first gig we ever played in London was to twenty-six people, and half of them went home before we were done. We laughed about it—we had to —but we never dreamed we'd be playing a sold-out show to six-thousand people three years later."

"Why not?"

"Because we're a pirate band from Derby. Shit like that doesn't happen to bands like us."

"Or so you thought."

"Yeah. I suppose." Shay could hear Ollie's slow, even breathing. It was nothing like the tense, snatched breaths he'd seen Ollie struggle for in darker conversations. "I think I need to unpick the journey, musically. We have so much material to choose from, it overwhelms me sometimes."

Ollie said nothing for a long moment. Then he sighed. "I over-shot the first film I was ever commissioned for. It was a three-minute movie, but I wound up with six hours of footage to break down."

"What did you do?"

"I deleted huge clips without looking at them, so I never really knew what I'd lost, but that's who I was back then—impulsive, selfish, and naive. If you don't know what you've lost, you can never learn."

They weren't talking about films and songs anymore. Shay white-knuckled his phone. "Where are you?"

It came out as a whisper. Perhaps Ollie wouldn't hear him.

But he did. Of course he did. "I'm at my mum's," Ollie said.

"After I left you, I came here for a few days. We had some stuff to work through."

"And did you? Work through it, I mean?"

"Getting there. It was more complicated than I thought it would be, but at the same time, so fucking simple, I don't know why it took me so long."

"Did you show her?"

Ollie snorted softly. "It wasn't *that* simple, mate. And no, I didn't show her, but it was never about that. My mum doesn't need to see shit to believe it. It's not as important as I made it sound… I know that now."

"Do you feel better?"

"Yeah. I do."

Shay wanted to know more. Fuck, he wanted to know it all, but perhaps that was Ollie's point. That the details didn't matter when the present was so important.

"Shay?"

"Yeah?"

"Thank you for the letter. You know I love you too, right?"

"Um… I think so?" Then Shay recalled every touch they'd ever shared, every smile and laugh, and he stood abruptly enough to shove the bench backwards. "Nah, I *know*. You don't have to say it, I know you love me, Ollie."

"Good," Ollie whispered. "Because I need you to know it, whatever happens. I do love you, and I don't know where I'd be headed if we hadn't met."

Shay couldn't imagine life without Ollie either. Barely a month had passed since they'd first laid eyes on each other, but the change in Shay was irrevocable. And he wouldn't have it any other way. All he needed was Ollie by his side, but instinct told him that wouldn't be happening any time soon. "You're not coming to the gig, are you?"

"No. I want to, but… not yet. You deserve the best of me, Shay, whoever that man is, and it's not the dude who freaks out every ten minutes about stupid things."

"None of it's stupid. Why are you so hard on yourself?"

"Because I have to be." Ollie spoke gently, his voice carrying none of the self-loathing Shay had heard from him before. "But not in the way you think. Sorry, mate, I know I talk like it's the end of the world all the time, but I don't feel like that… anymore."

Shay stretched his legs out in front of him. He still needed new boots. "I miss you."

"I miss you too. More than you know."

"Really?"

"Course I do. In between trying to put my brain back together, I've been setting up your final film. I can't be with you in London, but I'll be there in Leeds, I promise. There's something I need to put an end to here, and you deserve your beginning. Nothing can move forwards without it."

He was right. Shay knew it like he knew water was wet. And Leeds was so close he could taste it. He'd waited his whole life to meet Ollie. He could wait two days, right?

Shay picked up his flute. "Can I play you something before you go?"

CHAPTER TWENTY-FIVE

OLLIE HEARD Shay's flute in his sleep, but it didn't haunt him. Instead it bewitched him in all the right ways, keeping him company all night long.

The next morning, he listened to the recorded live stream of the last London gig, sitting at his mother's kitchen table with Shay's face spread over every available surface. After days of therapist appointments and soul-searching, he was finally ready to get back to work.

As ever, Shay consumed him, and he didn't hear Jannah come in until she was peering over his shoulder.

She drummed her fingers on the back of Ollie's chair, keeping perfect time with Larry's beat. "Is this your boyfriend?"

"He's not my boyfriend."

"But you want him to be?"

"Something like that."

Jannah tilted her head sideways, listening, and studied the still shots Ollie had printed out and spread over the tabletop. "He looks—"

Ollie held up his hand. "Don't say it."

"He doesn't know?"

Ollie thanked whoever for a mother who paid attention to the small stuff, even when he didn't want her to, and shook his head. "Not yet."

Jannah smiled. "He's beautiful."

"I know."

"I can see why you want to be better for him."

"It's not for him, it's for me."

"That's my boy."

Jannah left for work without a grand goodbye. Ollie was leaving too, for Leeds, to be with Shay, and he didn't know when he'd see his parents again. The last few days had been intense, but knowing it was limited had made it bearable. For the first time in years, he'd let them speak for him—to doctors and therapists. Now he was ready to speak for himself. *I need help, and I'm here to get it.*

Ollie's northbound train was leaving King's Cross late afternoon. All being well, he'd arrive in Leeds in time to catch the show.

At three o'clock, armed with the million mental health pamphlets he'd collected, he left his childhood home behind and took a cab across the city. The devil on his shoulder was louder than ever, but he'd learned new ways to quiet it over the last few days, methods and tools he'd need to practice to make them stick. His heart still pounded, and his hands trembled. But the cold sweat didn't come. *Winner.*

The traffic was a bitch, though. He caught the train by a whisker.

London to Birmingham New Street passed in a flash. Ollie worked the whole way, then ran to catch his connecting train. He found a seat with a table but didn't reopen his laptop. Apprehension and fear had been his constant companions for so long, the anticipation teasing his nerves was almost frightening.

But Ollie wasn't frightened. He was excited. In a few short hours, he'd be with Shay, and he couldn't fucking wait.

OLLIE STARED through the train window at the billowing smoke. If he squinted hard, he could make out the fierce flames breaking through the dying light of the day.

The train stopped, its path through the level crossing blocked by smoke. Blue lights battled for dominance with the orange glow as emergency vehicles surrounded the crash. Whatever happened, no one was going anywhere for a while.

Ollie fought hard to tear his gaze away, to hide from the fiery scene that was so reminiscent of the one he'd spent the last few days recounting he couldn't quite believe it. But he couldn't look away. He watched the firefighters get low and douse the upturned car with foam and water, watched the flames submit to a more powerful force, and searched for the meaning.

He didn't find it. But as the chaos cleared, he realised the car was empty. Saw the driver stood to one side, whole and unhurt, ruefully shaking his head.

Emotion akin to relief spread through Ollie. He turned away from the window and drew his legs up onto the seat. *If you'd looked away, you'd never have known the driver was safe. You'd have pictured him as burnt as you are for months and months, until you found something new to torment yourself with.*

The devil had been replaced by the straight-talking sibling he'd never had. Ollie swiped at his phone until he found Shay's face. His fingers hovered over the screen, but he didn't type. *Screw it.*

He pushed the phone aside, reached for his notebook, and began to write.

Shay,

So… I'm on the train on my way to Leeds and a car has crashed close to the tracks. We're stuck at the level crossing while they clear it, but the fire is out now. I stared at it for ages while it was burning. A week ago, I'd have hidden under the table, so I guess that's progress.

Fuck that. I know it is.

In case we don't get round to talking about it, I want you to know that I started therapy this week. It's not much, just an hour a week—in London, or online if I'm away—but it's something. It's everything, really, when I think about it. I learned yesterday that I've held on to my fear of cars, roads, fires… whatever it is, to protect me from reliving what happened. That it was easier to assume I was afraid of it than to accept it.

Go fucking figure. It's a thing, apparently.

I didn't believe it at first, but I do now, and I feel better just knowing. Because accepting what happened to me is easy. Unlearning years of unhealthy behaviour, thought patterns… yeah, that's harder. But I know I can do it.

Did I ever tell you I'm like a dog with a bone when I set my mind to something?

I hope I did. So you're not too surprised when it happens.

Anyway, I had three words planned for this note: gonna be late. I hope somewhere in my rambling I've made that clear….

I'll be late, but I'll be there.

I love you,

Ollie x

Ollie snapped a picture of the note and sent it to Shay. Then he turned his back on the accident scene, closed his eyes, and meditated himself to sleep.

Hours later, the train rolled into Leeds. The city was unfamiliar, but the alternative music club that was hosting Smuggler's Beat seemed to be everywhere. Billboards, bus stops. Ollie even spotted Shay's face on a recycling bin outside a KFC.

The pull to Shay was stronger than ever, so Ollie braved another cab. The tour bus was parked outside a hotel two streets away from the venue, dark and quiet. The gig was over, but the band were likely still clearing the stage. Or drinking. Or both.

Ollie swiped the door open and jogged up the steps. The bus was deserted save for a lone figure curled up on Ollie's bed.

Shay sat up, arms outstretched as though he'd been waiting for Ollie his whole damn life. "You're here."

Ollie smiled. "I am."

CHAPTER TWENTY-SIX

SHAY WOKE Ollie with silent kisses—his lips, his neck, lower. He wanted to dip his hands under Ollie's waistband and wake him with the kind of blow job that would send him straight back to sleep, but mindful of a bus full of sleeping bandmates, he settled for a quick squeeze.

Ollie groaned, cracked one eye open and then another. His gaze was as dark as ever, but the flinty edge that not even Shay had always managed to dodge was gone. The guardedness had left his slow, lazy grin, and he didn't seem entirely like Ollie at all.

What a difference a few days could make. Shay pictured Ollie's note—he'd committed it to memory—and tried to imagine what Ollie had been through to get to this point. But he couldn't, because Ollie was unimaginable. And Shay loved him for it.

They kissed. Ollie pulled Shay on top of him, letting him know without words exactly how much he might have appreciated Shay's first choice of a wake-up call.

Too soon, though, he drew back. "What time is it?"

"Nine."

"In the morning? Shit. I'm supposed to be somewhere in half an hour."

"Where?"

"A police station."

"Do I want to know why?"

Ollie shook his head. "Later, maybe."

Fuck. Shay had forgotten that today marked the last day of filming for the genealogy program. That if whatever had bloomed between him and Ollie hadn't happened, by the end of the day, Ollie would've been gone.

He sucked in a sharp breath. "Where am I supposed to be, and when?"

"Midday, and I'll text you a postcode. I need to finalise a couple of things this morning."

"How long will the filming take?"

Ollie shrugged. "I don't know, but whatever happens, we have to be back here by four. You've got some media shit to do in Derby tonight."

Shay wondered how, despite being MIA for days, Ollie knew Shay's schedule better than he did. Then he remembered he'd stopped paying attention to anything but the music. As ever, his brain danced away from the conversation and took him back to the show last night. After talking to Ollie about everything and nothing, he'd taken the set list back to the start—back to the days when the band had been nothing more than a flute and a drum kit. Track by track, he'd added layers to the show, culminating with a stomper they'd written on the road a few weeks ago that contained every instrument they'd had to hand. It was colour and chaos; it was the journey that brought them home.

And Shay had written the song with his gaze fixed on the back of Ollie's head.

"Hey." Ollie nudged him. "You want to go back to sleep for a while?"

Shay was tired enough from last night's show to sleep for a week, but he could handle it. Could handle anything while Ollie was lying on top him the way he was right now. "I'm good. Have you got time for breakfast?"

Ollie grinned. "Always."

"You brought me to a graveyard?"

Ollie spun around, camera in hand. He seemed surprised, though Shay was right on time. "Well, technically, you brought yourself. But yeah. Here we are."

"Should I be worried?"

"About what?"

"I don't know."

Ollie smiled a little and kissed Shay's cheek. For a long moment it was just them, but then he pulled back and shifted into what Shay recognised as his work mode. "I've set the tripod up over there." He pointed across to a far corner of the cemetery. "I'm going to go and fix the camera on it and set up the shot I want. When I signal, can you walk over?"

"Okay." Shay thrust his hands into his pockets and tracked Ollie as he made his way through the headstones. He shivered. After weeks of libraries and museums, the maudlin setting was unnerving. He glanced at the nearest inscription—a woman who'd died decades ago, but the grave was smothered in fresh flowers and plants, as though she'd been buried yesterday.

"Shay."

Dammit. Shay focused on Ollie. He'd missed the signal. Ollie shook his head and beckoned him over a second time, perhaps a third. Who the hell knew?

Shay followed the path through the cemetery until he came to the row where Ollie had set up the camera. The path faded there, and he had to step over graves to get to where Ollie was standing.

Another shot of nerves hit Shay hard. He stopped close to Ollie... close enough that their arms brushed. "Whose grave is this?"

"Take a look."

Shay turned to the sparse grave and studied the headstone. Rudek Nowack, 1966-1998. That was it, no loving messages or prayers, but it wasn't the brevity that caught Shay's attention. It was the name. "Nowack," he whispered. "That's my name."

Ollie squeezed Shay's arm. "It is. And Rudek is a derivative of Rudolph."

"So this is from the Danish side of the family? My mother's?"

"Actually, no. That you have relatives on both sides with variations of the name is a coincidence."

Shay read the name again. *Rudek Nowack.* Absorbed the dates, and gasped aloud. "He died in 1998. Who was he?"

Ollie's grip on Shay tightened. "He was your father."

<hr>

"HE WAS your father."

Shay had passed out more times than he cared to remember, but the way the earth moved when Ollie uttered those words was nothing like that. He grabbed Ollie's left arm, fingers digging in hard, forgetting to be mindful of Ollie's scars. "My father?"

"Yes."

"He's dead?"

"Yes." Ollie pried Shay's fingers from his arm and guided him away from the grave to a nearby bench. "I know his story, and your mother's, but it's not an easy one."

"I want to know."

"I know you do, but it doesn't have to be like this. I can turn the camera off and we can go someplace else."

"Like where?"

"Anywhere."

Shay shook his head. "The camera is why we're here—both of us. We need to finish the show."

Ollie didn't argue. But he gave Shay a moment while he dug a folder from the bag Shay hadn't noticed at his feet. When he straightened, he nodded. "Ready?"

"I'm ready."

Ollie held out a piece of paper. "This is a newspaper report from 1997. A woman, Ava Martin, went missing on her way home from work. Three days later, her body was found on Hawksworth Moor. She'd been murdered... by her ex-boyfriend."

Shay blew out a breath. "By my father?"

"Yes. He was tried and convicted and hung himself in Wake-field Prison not long after he received a life sentence."

My father was a murderer. Nausea roiled through Shay. His fingers tightened around the newspaper report, crumpling it.

Ollie took it away. "From what I understand, it wasn't a premeditated killing, but Rudek had multiple convictions for petty violence and drug offences. Ava had reported him for domestic violence more than once, but no charges had ever been filed."

"Was she my mother?"

"No."

"So who was?"

Ollie pressed another piece of paper into Shay's hands. A police report this time, dated six months before Ava Martin's death. A house fire on a Leeds housing estate. A twenty-six year old woman had died. Her name was Francesca King.

King. Shay's mind raced back over every name Ollie had ever given him. Joyce King, the woman who'd built ships in the Second World War had once been a Kaspersen. She'd married and had children... grandchildren. *Jesus Christ.* "Are you telling me my mother is dead too?"

"I'm sorry, Shay."

Shay sat back on the bench. The newspaper picture of Francesca King was grainy and blurred; he could hardly make her out, and for some reason, he was glad of it. The photographs of his relatives from centuries ago had excited him, his connection to them distant enough for curiosity to be his strongest emotion, even when he'd learned their fates.

This was different. These people were his parents... by blood, at least. "Do you know anything about Francesca?"

"A little," Ollie said. "She had no siblings, and her parents—your grandparents—are long dead, but she was an accomplished hockey player, so I've found some reports and stuff from when she was at school. Do you want to see them?"

"Maybe later." Shay cast his gaze back to his father's grave, chasing the missing links that had led to this point. "Where was I when the fire happened? Was I there?"

"Not as far as I can tell," Ollie said. "That's what I was checking this morning, an archived report of the fire. You would only have been a few months old, but there was no mention of a baby."

"But I was two when I was adopted, and I'd been in foster for only six months before that. What happened to me in between?"

Ollie bit his lip. "That's part of the reason I brought you here… more than for Rudek. I'm going to put the camera on the gimbal, okay? Then we're going to head over there."

Shay followed the jerk of Ollie's head to the back of the grave-yard. "To the trees?"

"Yeah. Just give me a sec."

Shay couldn't wait. Ollie briefly forgotten, he rose from the bench and drifted to the back of the cemetery. There were no graves there, only trees of varying ages, plaques and tablets, and a couple of benches. Memorials. Shay scanned every name until his breath caught.

In memory of Artur and Zofia Nowack. Fly high, we loved you.

Shay wavered again. Ollie was there, his hands steady and strong. Shay clung to him. "Who were they?"

"Your grandparents. Rudek's parents. They cared for you after Francesca died. Fought for you. But for whatever reason, probably something to do with Rudek, social services wouldn't let them keep you. You were taken from them and put into foster care. As far as I can tell, you never saw them again."

"But they wanted me?"

"Yes, Shay. They did, very much."

"Where are they buried if not here?"

Ollie drew Shay away from the willow tree someone had planted in honour of his grandparents. Another bench was a heartbeat away. They sat, knees pressed together, hands clasped. Shay belatedly realised the camera was nowhere to be seen, but he didn't care enough to ask why.

He gripped Ollie's hands hard enough to bend bones. "Finish the story."

Ollie was silent for a moment that seemed to last a lifetime, then he fixed Shay with his patented endless stare. "Your grandparents came to this country in the sixties. They settled in London and took over a cafe in Vauxhall. They ran it for years... it was only sold a few years ago, but their children—two sons—left the city sometime in the eighties. Both of them wound up in Leeds, for cheaper housing, I'd imagine, but I don't know for sure."

"What happened next?"

"Well, your grandparents continued to run the cafe together until your grandmother, Zofia, became too frail. She went into a home in Pimlico, where she died a few years ago." Ollie paused a beat. "After she went into the home, Artur ran the cafe with the help of his grandson... your cousin. But they sold up a little while before Zofia died, and when she was gone, Artur took her home."

Home. "Where, Ollie? Where was home?"

"Warsaw." Ollie squeezed Shay's hands ever tighter. "Your grandparents are buried a mile away from my family home."

"I'm Polish?"

Ollie's smile was cautious. "Yes, Shay. You are."

"Tell me what it's called."

"What?"

"The *Polish* instrument you gave me."

Ollie's smile widened a touch. "It's a hurdy-gurdy, and I found a photograph in an old London newspaper of Artur playing it. Would you like to see?"

Shay stared at Ollie as though seeing him for the first time. His black hair seemed darker, his stormy eyes somehow bluer. "Is that a real question?"

"No. I have it right here."

Of course he did. Ollie had everything Shay would ever need.

EPILOGUE

Six months later....

"I THINK I should start calling myself Rudzio."

Ollie glanced up from his laptop. Shay was sitting on the patio in his garden, barefoot and shirtless, apparently writing, though he seemed to be staring into space more than playing the Polish hurdy-gurdy he'd fast mastered now he knew what it was and where it came from. "You want to use your Polish name?"

"Not really... but I think Rudzio Maloney is a cool moniker for a performer."

"Not Rudzio Nowack?"

"Nah. It's not my name to use. Besides, I can't be all of one and none of the other."

That made sense. Shay had spent a long time coming to terms with his family history, but he'd never travelled far from the people who'd raised him. He'd always be a Maloney, and he'd chosen not to seek out any surviving members of his biological family... for now.

Shay went back to ruminating, and Ollie went back to approving the final edits on the genealogy documentary they'd filmed on the road. The Smuggler's Beat tour seemed to Ollie as though it had happened a week ago. It was hard to imagine Shay was gearing up for another.

The final frames passed across Ollie's screen. He'd cut the footage himself, but a second editor, a fresh pair of eyes, had reworked it so Ollie featured more than he wanted to. The last scene showed him and Shay from a distance, huddled up on a bench, heads bowed, hands clasped.

Ollie recalled their exchange in that moment, word for word.

"I'm Polish?"

"Yes, Shay. You are."

But more than that, he remembered Shay's blinding smile. Remembered returning it and hugging Shay so tight neither one of them could breathe. Shay's backstory was tragic, but that they shared a heritage, and it mattered so much to Shay, was more than Ollie had ever dared dream.

He shut his laptop and wandered outside. The summer sun was beating down in Shay's cottage garden. Ollie's scars, exposed by his ripped T-shirt, tingled, but it no longer frightened him. He revelled in it, and Shay's lithe, bare body called to him. He held out his hands. "Come here."

Shay took his hands and stood. "I know that look."

"Of course you do. You know everything about me."

"Is that a bad thing?"

"No. I like it."

"Why?"

It was so Shay to ask that question and to be fascinated by the answer. Ollie kissed his lips, lightly at first, then harder, before pulling away to consider his answer. "Because it opens me up. I can see outside myself when I know you've seen the inside."

It didn't make much sense, but Shay didn't care about shit like that. He loved Ollie, and Ollie loved him. Anything Ollie said was enough. Always.

Ollie tugged Shay inside and upstairs. Shay's bedroom—*their* bedroom when they weren't in London—was in the attic and contained nothing but a guitar and a king-size bed. Shay let Ollie back him against it and push him down. Already half-dressed, he didn't protest as Ollie yanked his jeans down and tossed them away.

His bright gaze holding Ollie prisoner, he rose up on his knees and grasped Ollie's T-shirt. He pulled it up slowly, giving Ollie every chance to stop him. But Ollie didn't stop him. He never had. And the instinct to even think about it was fading with every passing day.

Shay threw Ollie's T-shirt... somewhere. The rest of Ollie's clothes followed, and then he lay back on the bed and coaxed Ollie on top of him. He bit Ollie's jaw, his cheek, his ear. "Fuck me. I know you want to."

Want. Need. Ollie no longer knew the difference when it came to Shay. He flipped Shay over so he was on his stomach and eased inside him for only the second time ever. The first had been drunken and filthy, but it was different now. They were the same, but different. Always moving forwards, but never forgetting the past.

Sensation took over and Ollie fucked Shay until they both cried out, trembling as if they were one soul, joined, irrevocably, in every possible way.

Shay gasped for breath, fisting the sheets. For a long moment, it seemed to Ollie as though they'd be coming forever, but then it was over, and they were left with cooling sweat and laughter.

Ollie helped Shay roll over. "Okay?"

Shay grinned. "Yeah. I've been dreaming of that all day."

"Just all day?"

"Shut up."

Ollie took him at his word and collapsed beside him, craving a postcoital snooze. He let his eyes fall closed and drifted, but a sharp poke to his ribs dragged him back.

He opened his eyes to find Shay's face an inch from his. "What's up?"

"Nothing." Shay pushed his sex-tousled hair out of his eyes. "I didn't want you to go to sleep without telling you I love you."

"You think I don't know?"

"Nah, I know you know, but I'll never get tired of saying it."

How did we get here? They'd fallen in love in the space of a few short weeks—Ollie had most of it on film, the rest indelibly marked on his heart, but sometimes he couldn't quite believe any of it. How they'd come from the edge of nowhere to the top of a world they'd built for themselves. He stretched up and captured Shay's addictive lips in a bruising kiss. "I'll never get tired of hearing it, and for the record, I love you too. More than you'll ever know."

"Good. Because I still need new boots."

FURTHER READING

Curious about Shay's cousin? The grandparents who fought so hard for him? Sam's love story can be found in What Matters.

Lucky Man is is the story of Finn McGovern, and in this book you will also find Ben.

NEWSLETTER

Get a free story!

For the most up to date news and free books, subscribe to my newsletter HERE.

This is a zero spam zone. Maximum number of emails you will receive is one per month.

PATREON

Not ready to let go of Shay and Ollie? Or looking for sneak peeks at future books in the series? Alternative POVs, outtakes, and missing moments from **all** Garrett's books can be found on her Patreon site. Misfits, Slide, Strays…the works. Because you know what? Garrett wasn't ready to let her boys go either.

Pledges start from as little as $2, and all content is available at the lowest tier.

ABOUT GARRETT LEIGH

Bonus Material available for all books on Garrett's Patreon account. Includes short stories from Misfits, Slide, Strays, What Remains, Dream, and much more. Sign up here: https://www.patreon.com/garrettleigh

Facebook Fan Group, Garrett's Den... https://www.facebook.com/groups/garre...

Garrett Leigh is an award-winning British writer, cover artist, and book designer. Her debut novel, Slide, won Best Bisexual Debut at the 2014 Rainbow Book Awards, and her polyamorous novel, Misfits was a finalist in the 2016 LAMBDA awards, and was again a finalist in 2017 with Rented Heart.

In 2017, she won the EPIC award in contemporary romance with her military novel, Between Ghosts, and the contemporary romance category in the Bisexual Book Awards with her novel What Remains.

When not writing, Garrett can generally be found procrastinating on Twitter, cooking up a storm, or sitting on her behind doing as little as possible, all the while shouting at her menagerie of children and animals and attempting to tame her unruly and wonderful FOX.

Garrett is also an award winning cover artist, taking the silver medal at the Benjamin Franklin Book Awards in 2016. She designs for various publishing houses and independent authors at blackjazzdesign.com, and co-owns the specialist stock site moonstock-photography.com

Connect with Garrett
www.garrettleigh.com